I0756441

The Autobiography *of Methuselah*

The Autobiography *of Methuselah*

John Kendrick Bangs

Ægypan Press

1908

Special thanks to David Clarke, Sankar Viswanathan, and the Online Distributed Proofreading Team (which can be found at http://www.pgdp.net). Thanks also to Internet Archive/American Libraries (which can be found at http://www.archive.org/details/americana).

The Autobiography of Methuselah
A publication of
ÆGYPAN PRESS

www.aegypan.com

Foreword

Having recently passed into what my great-grandson Shem calls my Anecdotage, it has occurred to me that perhaps some of the recollections of a more or less extended existence upon this globular* mass of dust and water that we are pleased to call the earth, may prove of interest to posterity, and I have accordingly, at the earnest solicitation of my grandson, Noah, and his sons, Shem, Ham and Japhet, consented to put them into permanent literary form. In view of the facts that at this writing, ink and paper and pens have not as yet been invented, and that we have no capable stenographers among our village folk, and that because

* It is quite interesting, in the light of the contentions of history as to man's earliest realization that the earth is round, to find Methuselah speaking in this fashion. It would seem from this that the real facts had dawned upon the Patriarch's mind even at this early period, and one is therefore disposed to regard as less apocryphal the anecdote recorded in Volume III, Chapter 38, of "The Life and Voyages of Noah," wherein Adam, after being ejected from the Garden of Eden, asked by Cain if he believes the world to be round like an orange, replies:

"I used to think so, my son, but under prevailing conditions I am forced into a more or less definite suspicion that it is elliptical, like a lemon." – Editor

of my advanced years I should find great difficulty in producing my manuscript on a type-writing machine with my gouty fingers – for, of the luscious fluid of the grape have I been a ready, though never overabundant, consumer – even if I were familiar with the keyboard of such an instrument, or, if indeed, there were any such instrument to facilitate the work – in view of these facts, I say, I have been compelled to make use of the literary methods of the Egyptians, and with hammer and chisel, to gouge out my "Few Remarks" upon such slabs of stone as I can find upon my native heath.

Let us hope that my story will not prove as heavy as my manuscript. It is hardly necessary for me to assure the indulgent reader that such a method of composition is not altogether an easy task for a man who is shortly to celebrate his nine hundred and sixty-fifth birthday, more especially since at no time in my life have I studied the arts of the Stone-Cutter, or been a master in the Science of Quarrying. Nor is it easy at my advanced age, with a back no longer sinewy, and muscles grown flabby from lack of active exercise, for me to lift a virgin sheet of stone from the ground to the surface of my writing-desk without a derrick, but these are, after all, minor difficulties, and I shall let no such insignificant obstacles stand between me and the great purpose I have in mind. I shall persist in the face of all in the writing of this Autobiography if for no worthier object than to provide occupation for my leisure hours which, in these patriarchal days to which I have attained, sometimes hang heavy on my hands. I know not why it should so transpire, but it is the fact that since I passed my nine hundred and fiftieth birthday I have had little liking for the pleasures which modern society most affects. To be sure, old and feeble as I am, and despite the uncertain quality of my knees,

I still enjoy the excitement of the Virginia Reel, and can still hold my own with men several centuries younger than myself in the clog, but I leave such diversions as bridge, draw-poker and pinochle to more frivolous minds – though I will say that when my great-grandchildren, Shem, Ham and Japhet, the sons of my grandson Noah, come to my house on the few holidays, their somewhat oversober parent allows them from their labors in the ship-yard, I take great delight in sitting upon the ground with them and renewing my acquaintance with those games of my youth, marbles, and mumblety-peg, the which I learned from my great-uncle-seven-times-removed, Cain, in the days when with my grandfather, Jared, I used to go to see our first ancestor, Adam, at the old farm just outside of Edensburg where, with his beautiful wife Eve, that Grand Old Man was living in honored retirement.

Nor have I in these days, as I used to have, any especial taste for the joys of the chase. There was a time when my slungshot was unerring, and I could bring down a Dodo, or snipe my Harpy on the wing with as much ease as my wife can hit our barn-door with a rolling-pin at six feet, and for three hundred and thirty years I never let escape me any opportunity for tracking the Dinosaur, the Pterodactyl, or that fierce and sanguinary creature the Osteostogothemy to his lair and there fighting him unto the death during the open season for wild game of that particular sort. I well remember how, in my boyhood days, to be precise, shortly after my two hundred and twenty-second birthday, I went with my great-grandfather, Mehalaleel, over into the woods back of Little Ararat after a great horned Ornythyrhyncus and – but that is another story. Suffice it to say that I have at last reached a period in my life where I am content to leave the pleasures of Nimrod to my more nimble neighbors, and that now no winged thing, save an occasional mosquito, or locust, need fear my approach, and that my indulgence in the shedding of the blood of animals is confined to an infrequent personal superintendence of the slaughter of a spring-lamb in green-pea time, when the scent is in the julep and the bloom is on the mint; or possibly, now and then, the removal from the pasture to the pantry of a bit of lowing roast-beef, when I feel an inner craving for the crackle and the steak.

Racing I have an abhorrence for, and always have had since in my early days I attended the county-fair at North Ararat, and was there induced by one of my neighbors to participate as a rider in a twenty-mile steeplechase between a Discosaurus which I rode, and a Diplodocus in his possession. I found after the race had started that the animal which had been assigned to me as a gentleman jockey, had not been broken to the saddle, and my experience during the next six days in staying on his back – for he immediately took the bit between his teeth and bolted for the woods, and was not again got under control for that time – as he jumped over the various obstacles to his progress, from thank-you-marms in the highways which were plentiful, to such mountains as the country for a thousand miles about provided for his delectation, was one of the most terrific in my life, prolonged as it has been. I had been assured that the race was to be a "Go-As-You-Please" affair, but I had not been seated on that horrible creature's back for two minutes before I discovered that it was a "Go-As-He-Pleased" affair and that "Going-As-I-Pleased," like the flowers that bloom in the Spring, had nothing to do with the case. Had I begun in the pursuit of the pleasures of the track in later years after the invention of wheels, whereby that easy running vehicle, the sulky, was brought into being, and when, by the taming of the horse, the latter became a domesticated animal with sporting proclivities, instead of a mere prowler of the plains, I might have found the joys of racing more to my taste, although in these later years of my life when a truly noble pursuit has degenerated into a mere gambling enterprise, wherein those who can ill afford it squander their substance in riotous bookmaking, I am inclined to be grateful that my first experience in this direction has led me to cultivate an unconcerned aloofness from a pursuit which is ruinous to the old and corrupting to the young.

Were the present state of literature more hopeful, perhaps I should find pleasure in reading, but I have viewed with such increasing alarm the growth of sensationalism in the literary output of my age that I have felt that I owed it to my posterity, which is rapidly growing in numbers – I believe that the latest annual report of the Society of the Sons and Daughters of Methuselah shows a membership of six hundred and thirty-eight thousand, without counting the new arrivals since the end of the last fiscal year, which, at a rough guess, I should place at thirty-six thousand – I have felt, I say, that I owe it to that posterity to set it the example of not reading, as my most effective protest against those pernicious influences which have made the modern literary school a menace to civilization. Surely if Noah's children for instance, Shem, Ham and Japhet, whom I have already had occasion to mention, were to surprise me, their venerable, and I hope venerated ancestor, reading such stories as are now put forth by our most successful quarrymen – stories like that unspeakable novel "Three Decades," of which I am credibly informed eight million tons have already been sold; and which, let me say, when I had read only seven slabs of it I had carted away and dumped into the Red Sea; or the innocuous but highly frivolous tales of Miss Laura Jean Diplodocus – they would hardly accept from me as worthy of serious attention such admonitions as I am constantly giving them on the subject of the decadence of literature when I find them poring over the novels of the day. Consequently even this usual solace of old age is denied to me, and writing becomes my refuge.

I bespeak the reader's indulgence if he or she find in the ensuing pages any serious lapses from true literary style. I write merely as I feel, and do not pretend to be either an expert hieroglyphist or a rhetorician of commanding quality. Perhaps I should do more wisely if I were to accept the advice of my great-grandson Ham, who, overhearing my remark to a caller last Sunday evening that the work I have undertaken is one of considerable difficulty, climbed up into my lap and in his childish way asked me why I did not hire a boswell to do it for me. I had to tell the child that I did not know what a boswell was, and when I questioned him on the subject more closely, I found that it was only one of his childish fancies. If there were such a thing as that rather euphoniously named invention of Ham's who could relieve me of the drudgery of writing my own life, and who would do it well, I would cheerfully relinquish that end of my enterprise to him, but in the absence of such a thing, I am, in spite of my manifest shortcomings, compelled to do the work myself. On behalf of my story I can say, however, that whatever I shall put down here will be the truth, and that what I remember notwithstanding my advanced years, I remember perfectly. I am quite aware that in some of the tales that I shall tell, especially those having to do with Prehistoric Animals I have met, or Antediluvians as I believe the Scientists call them, what I may say as to their habits – I was going to say manners, but refrain because in all my life I have never observed that they had any – and powers may fall upon some ears as extravagant exaggerations. To these let me say here and now that there are exceptions to all rules, and that if for instance, I tell the story of a Pterodactyl that after being swallowed whole by a Discosaurus, successfully gnaws his way through the walls of the latter's stomach to freedom, I make no claim that all Pterodactyls could do the same, but merely that in this particular case the Pterodactyl to which I refer did it, and that I know that he did it because the man who saw it is a cousin of my grandfather's first wife's step-son, and is so wedded to truth that he is even now in jail because he would not deny a charge of sheep-stealing, which he might easily have done were he an untruthful man. Again when I observe that I have caught with an ordinary fish-hook, baited with a common garden, or angle worm, on the end of a light trout-line, a Creosaurus with a neck ninety-seven feet long, and scales so large that you could weigh a hay-wagon on the smallest of the lot near the end of his tail, I admit at the outset that the feat was unusual, had never occurred before, and is never likely to occur again, but can bring affidavits to prove that it did happen that time, signed by reputable parties who have heard me tell about it more than once. I make these statements here not in any sense to apologize for anything I shall say in my book, but merely to forestall the criticism of highly cultivated and truly scientific readers who, after a lifelong study of the habits of these creatures may feel impelled to question the accuracy of my statements and add to my perplexities by so advertising my book that I shall be put to the arduous necessity of chiseling out another edition, a labor which I have no desire to assume.

One word more as to the language I have chosen for the presentation of my narrative. I have chosen English as the language in which to chisel out these random recollections of mine for a variety of reasons. Most conspicuous of these is that at the time of this writing no one has as yet thought to devise a French, German, Spanish or Italian language. Russian I have no familiarity with. Chinese I do not care for. Latin and Greek few people can read, and as for Egyptian, while it is an excellent and fluent tongue for speaking purposes, I find myself appalled at the prospect of writing a story of the length of mine in the hieroglyphics which up to date form the whole extent of Egyptian chirography. An occasional pictorial rebus in a child's magazine is a source of pleasure and profit to both the young and the old, but the autobiography of a man of my years told in pictures, and pictures for the most part of squab, spring chickens, and canvas-back ducks, would, I fear, prove arduous reading. Moreover I am but an indifferent draftsman, and I suspect that when the precise thought that I have in mind can best be expressed by a portrait of a hummingbird, or a flamingo, my readers because of my inexpert handling of my tools would hardly be able to distinguish the creature I should limn from an albatross, a red-head duck, or a June-Bug, which would lead to a great deal of obscurity, and in some cases might cause me to say things that I should not care to be held responsible for. There is left me then only a choice between English and Esperanto, and I incline to the former, not because I do not wish the Esperantists well, but because in the present condition of the latter's language, it affects the eye more like a barbed-wire fence than a medium for the expression of ideas.

At this stage of the proceedings I can think of nothing else either to explain or to apologize for, but in closing I beg the reader to accept my assurance that if in the narratives that follow he finds anything that needs either explanation or apology, I shall be glad to explain if he will bring the matter to my attention, and herewith tender in advance for his acceptance any apology which occasion may require.

And so to my story.

George W. Methuselah
Ararat Corners, B.C. 2348

Chapter I

I AM BORN AND NAMED

The date of my birth, occurring as it did, nine hundred and sixty-five years ago, is so far removed from my present that my recollections of it are not altogether clear, but Mrs. Adam, my great-grandmother seven times removed, with whom I was always a great favorite because I looked more like my original ancestor, her husband, than any other of his descendants, has given me many interesting details of that important epoch in my history. Personally I do remember that the date was B. C. 3317, and the twenty-third of June, for the first thing to greet my infant eyes, when I opened them for the first time, was a huge insurance calendar hanging upon our wall whereon the date was printed in letters almost as large as those which the traveling circuses of Armenia use to herald the virtues of their show when at County Fair time they visit Ararat Corners. I also recall that it was a very stormy day when I arrived. The rain was coming down in torrents, and I heard simultaneously with my arrival my father, Enoch, in the adjoining room making sundry observations as to the meteorological conditions which he probably would have spoken in a lower tone of voice, or at least in less vigorous phraseology had he known that I was within earshot, although I must confess that it has always been a nice question with me whether or not when a man expresses a wish that the rain may be dammed, he voices a desire for its everlasting condemnation, or the mere placing in its way of an impediment which shall prevent its further overflow. I think much depends upon the manner, the inflection, and the tone of voice in which the desire is expressed, and I am sorry to say that upon the occasion to which I refer, there was more of the asperity of profanity than the calmness of constructive suggestion in my father's manner. In any event I did not blame him, for here was I coming along, undeniably imminent, a tempest raging, and no doctor in sight, and consequently no telling when my venerable sire would have to go out into the wet and fetch one.

In those primitive days doctors were few and far between. There was little profit in the practice of such a profession at a time when everybody lived so long that death was looked upon as a remote possibility, and one seldom called one in until after he had passed his nine hundredth birthday and sometimes not even then. It may be that this habit of putting off the call to the family physician was the cause of our wonderful longevity, but of that I do not know, and do not care to express an opinion on the subject, for socially I have always found the medicine folk charming companions and I would not say aught in this work that could by any possibility give them offense. Not only were doctors rare at that period, but owing to our limited facilities in the matter of transportation, it was exceedingly difficult for them to get about. The doctor's gig, now so generally in use, had not as yet been brought to that state of perfection that has made its use in these modern times a matter of ease and comfort. We had wheels, to be sure, but they were not spherical as they have since become, and were made out of stone blocks weighing ten or fifteen tons apiece, and hewn octagonally, so that a ride over the country roads in a vehicle of that period not only involved the services of some thirty or forty horses to pull the wagon, but an endless succession of jolts which, however excellent they may have been in their influence on the liver were most trying to the temper, and resulted in attacks of sickness which those who have been to sea tell me strongly resembles sea-sickness. So rough indeed was the operation of riding in the wagons of my early youth that a great many of our best people who kept either horses or domesticated elephants, still continued to drive about in stone boats, so-called, built flat like a raft, rather than suffer the shaking up which the new-fangled wheels entailed. Griffins were also used by persons of adventurous nature, but were gradually dying into disuse, and the species being no longer bred becoming extinct, because of the great difficulty in domesticating them. It was not a hard task to break them to the saddle, and on the ground they were fleet and sure footed, but in the air they were extremely unreliable. They used their wings with much power, but were not responsive to the reins, and in flying pursued the most erratic courses. What was worse, they were seldom able to alight after an aërial flight on all four feet at once, having a disagreeable habit of approaching the earth vertically, and headfirst, so that the rider, unless he were strapped on, was usually unseated while forty or fifty feet in the air, with the result that he either broke his neck, or at least four or five ribs, and a leg or two, at the end of his ride. When we remember that in addition to all this we had no telephone service at that time, and that the umbrella had not as yet been devised, my father's anxiety at the moment may easily be realized.

His temper was only momentary, however, for I recall that I was very much amused at this critical moment of my career by another observation that I overheard from the adjoining room. My grandfather, Jared, who was with my father at the time looking out of the window made the somewhat commonplace observation –

"It's raining cats and dogs, isn't it?"

"Cats and dogs?" retorted Enoch, scornfully. "It's raining Diplodocuses!"

This was naturally the first bit of humor that I had ever heard, and coming as it did simultaneously with my début as a citizen of Enochsville, perhaps it is not to be wondered at that instead of celebrating my birth with a squall, as do most infants, I was born laughing. I must have cackled pretty loudly, too, for the second thing that I remember – O, how clearly it all comes back to me as I write, or rather chisel – was overhearing the Governor's response to the nurse's announcement of my arrival.

"It's a boy, sir," the good woman called out as she rushed excitedly into the other room.

"Good, Dinah," replied my father. "You have taken a great load off my mind. I am dee-lighted. I was afraid from his opening remarks that he was a hen!"

It was thus that the keynote of existence was struck for me, one of mirth even in the dark of storm, and that I have since become the oldest man that ever lived, and shall doubtless continue to the end of time to hold the record for longevity, I attribute to nothing else than that, thanks to my father's droll humor, I was born smiling. Nor did the good old gentleman ever stint himself in the indulgence of that trait. In my youth such things as comic papers were entirely unknown, nor did the columns of the newspapers give over any portion of their space to the printing of jokes, so that my dear old father never dreamed of turning his wit to the advantage of his own pocket, as do some latter-day joke-wrights who shall be nameless, lavishly bestowing the fruits of his gift upon the members of his own family. Of my own claims to an inheritance of humor from my sire, I shall speak in a later chapter.

I recall that my first impressions of life were rather disappointing. I cannot say that upon my arrival I brought with me any definite notions as to what I should find the world to be like, but I do know that when I looked out of the window for the first time it seemed to me that the scenery was rather commonplace, and the mountains which I could see in the distance, were not especially remarkable for grandeur. The rivers, too, seemed trite. That they should flow down-hill struck me as being nothing at all remarkable, for I could not for the life of me see how they could do otherwise, and when night came on and my nurse, Dinah, pointed out the moon and asked me if I did not think it was remarkable, I was so filled with impatience that so ordinary a phenomenon should be considered unusual that I made no reply whatsoever, smiling inwardly at the marvelous simplicity of these people with whom destiny had decreed that I should come to dwell. I should add, however, that I was quite contented on that first day of my existence for the reason that all of my wants appeared to be anticipated by my guardians, the table was good, and all through the day I was filled with a comfortable sense of my own importance as the first born of one of the first families of the land, and when along about noon the skies cleared, and the rain disappeared before the genial warmth of the sun, and the neighbors came in to look me over, it was most agreeable to realize that I was the center of so much interest. What added to my satisfaction was the fact that when my great-uncle Zib came in and began to talk baby-talk to me – a jargon that I have always abhorred – by an apparently casual movement of my left leg I was able with seeming innocence of intention to kick him on the end of his nose.

An amusing situation developed itself along about 4 o'clock in the afternoon, in respect to my name. One of the neighbors asked my father what my name was to be.

"Well," he replied with a chuckle, "we are somewhat up a tree in respect to that. We have held several family conclaves on the subject, and after much prayerful consideration of the matter we had finally settled on Gladys, but – well, since we've seen him the idea has been growing on us that he looks more like a James."

And indeed this question as to my name became a most serious one as the days passed by, and at one time I began to fear that I should be compelled to pass through life anonymously. There was some desire on the part of my father, who was of a providential nature, to call me Zib, after my great uncle of that name, for Uncle Zib had been forehanded, and was possessed of much in the way of filthy lucre, owning many cliff-dwellings, a large if not controlling interest in the Armenian Realty Company, whose caves on the leading thoroughfares of Enochsville and Edensburg commanded the highest and steadiest rents, and was the chief stock-holder in the Ararat Corners and Red Sea Traction Company, running an hourly service of Pterodactyls and Creosauruses between the most populous points of the country. This naturally made of Uncle Zib a nearer approach to a Captain of Finance than anything else known to our time, and inasmuch as he had never married, and was without an heir, my father thought he would appreciate the compliment of having his first-born named for him. But Uncle Zib's moral character was of such a nature that his name seemed to my mother as hardly a fit association for an infant of my tender years. He was known to be addicted to pinochle to a degree that had caused no end of gossip at the Ararat Woman's Club, and before he had reached the age of three hundred he had five times been successfully sued in the courts for breach of promise. Indeed, if Uncle Zib had had fewer material resources he would long since have been ostracized by the best people of our section, and even as it was the few people in our neighborhood to whom he had not lent money regarded his social pretensions with some coolness. The fact that he had given Enochsville a public library, and had filled its shelves with several tons of the best reading that the Egyptian writers of the day provided, was regarded as a partial atonement for some of his indiscretions, and the endowment of a large stone-quarry at Ararat where children were taught to read and write, helped materially in his rehabilitation, but on the whole Uncle Zib was looked upon askance by the majority. On the other hand Uncle Azag, a strong, pious man, who owed money to everybody in town, was the one after whom my mother wished me to be named, a proposition which my father resisted to the uttermost expense of his powers.

"What's the use?" I heard him ask, warmly. "He'll get his name on plenty of I.O.U.'s on his own account before he leaves this glad little earth, without our giving him an autograph that is already on enough overdue paper to decorate every flat in Uncle Zib's model tenements."

The disputation continued with some acrimony for a week, until finally my father put his foot down.

"I'm tired of referring to him as IT," he blurted out one night. "We'll compromise, and name him after me and thee. He shall be called Me for me, and Thou for thee, Selah!"

And so it was that from that day forth I was known as Methouselah, since corrupted into Methuselah.

Chapter II

EARLY INFLUENCES

Boys remained boys in those old days very much longer than they do now. The smartness of children like my grandsons, Shem, Ham and Japhet, for instance, who at the age of two hundred and fifty arrogate to themselves all the knowledge of the universe, was comparatively unknown when I was a child. To begin with we were of a different breed from the boys of today, and life itself was more simple. We were surrounded with none of those luxuries which are characteristic of modern life, and we were in no haste to grow old by taking short cuts across the fields of time. We were content to remain youthful, and even childish, taking on ourselves none of the superiorities of age until we had attained to the years which are presumed to go with discretion. We did not think either arrogantly or otherwise that we knew more by intuition than our parents had been able to learn from experience, and, with a few possible exceptions, we none of us assumed that position of high authority in the family which is, I regret to say, generally assumed by the sons and daughters of the present. For myself, I was quite willing to admit, even on the day of my birth, that my father, in spite of certain obvious limitations, knew more than I; and that my mother in spite of the fact that she was a woman, was possessed, in a minor degree perhaps, but still indubitably possessed, of certain of the elementary qualities at least of human intelligence. As I recall my attitude towards my elders in those days, the only person whose pretensions to superior attainments along lines of universal knowledge I was at all inclined to resent, was my maiden aunt, Jerusha, my father's sister, who, having attained to the kittenish age of 623 years, unmarried, and having consequently had no children, knew more about men and their ways, and how to bring up children scientifically than anybody at that time known to civilized society. Indeed I have always thought that it was the general recognition of the fact that Aunt Jerusha knew just a little more than there was to know that had brought about that condition of enduring spinsterhood in which she was passing her days. Even her, however, I could have viewed with amused toleration if so be she could have been induced to practice her theories as to the Fifty-seven Best Ways To Bring Up The Young upon others than myself. She was an amusing young thing, and the charming way in which even in middle age – she was as I have already said 623 years old at the time of which I write – she held on to the manners of youth was delightful to contemplate. She always kept herself looking very fit, and was the first woman in our section of the world to wear her hair pompadour in front, running to the extreme psychic knot behind – she called it psychic, though I have since learned that the proper adjective is Psyche, indicating rather a levity of mind than anything else. It should be said of her in all justice that she was a leader in her set, and as President of the Woman's Club of Enochsville was a person of more than ordinary influence, and it was through her that the movement to grant the franchise to all single women over three hundred and forty, resulted in the extension of the suffrage to that extent.

Incidentally I cannot forget the wise words of my father in this connection. He had always been an anti-suffragist, but when Aunt Jerusha's plan was laid before him he swung instantly around and became one of its heartiest advocates.

"It is a wise measure," said he. "Safe, sane and practical, for no single woman will confess to the age of qualification, so that in passing this act we grant the prayers of our petitioners without subjecting ourselves to the dangers of women's suffrage. Remember my son, that it always pays to be generous with that which costs you nothing, and that woman's suffrage is as harmless as the cooing dove if you only take the precaution to raise the age limit high enough to freeze out the old maids."

I should add too that Aunt Jerusha had a way with her that was not without its fascination. To look at her you would never have supposed that she was more than four hundred years old, and the variety of eyes that she could make when there were men about, was wonderful to see. I noticed it the very day I was born, and when I first caught sight of that piquante little glance that now and then she cast in my direction out of the tail of her eye, I began rummaging about in the back of my subconscious mind for the precise words with which to characterize her.

"You giddy old flirt!" was the apostrophe I had in mind at the moment, but, of course, having had no practice in speech I was compelled to forego the pleasure of giving audible expression to the thought.

Unfortunately for me Aunt Jerusha equipped with that intuitive knowledge of what to do under any given circumstances that invariably goes with the status of maiden-aunthood in its acute stages, now assumed complete control of my destinies; and for a time it looked as though I were in a fair way to become what the great Egyptian ruler, King Ptush the Third was referring to in many of his State papers as a "Meticulous Mollycoddle." To begin with, Aunt Jerusha was a strong believer in the New Thought School of Infantile Development, and when I was barely six weeks old she began strapping me on a board like an Eskimo baby, and suspending me thus restrained to a peg in the wall, where, helpless, I was required to hang and stare while she implanted the germs of strength in my soul by reading aloud whole chapters from the inspired chiselings of the popular seer Ber Nard Pshaw, who was to the literature of that period what King Ptush was to statecraft. He was the acknowledged leader of the Neo-Bunkum School of Right Thinking, and had first attracted the attention of his age by his famous reply to one who had called him an Egotist.

"I am more than that," he answered. "I am a Megotist. The world is full of I's, but there is only one Me."

Upon this sort of thing was I fed, not only spiritually but physically, by my Aunt Jerusha. When, for instance, I found myself suffering from a pain in my Commissary Department for the sole and sufficient reason that my nurse had inadvertently handed me the hard cider jug instead of my noon-day bottle of discosaurus' milk, she would rattle off some such statement as this: *Thought is everything. Pain is something. Hence where there is no thought there can be no pain. Wherefore if you have a pain it is evident that you have a thought. To be rid of the pain stop thinking.*

Then she would fix her eye on mine, and gaze at me sternly in an effort to remove my sufferings by the hot poultice of her own mushy reflections instead of getting the peppermint and the hot-water bag. When night came on and I was restless instead of wooing slumber on my behalf with soft and soothing lullabies, or telling me fairy-stories such as children love, she would say: *The child's mind is immature. His conclusions, therefore, are immature. Whence his decisions as to what he likes lack maturity, and consequently to give him that for which he professes to like is equivalent to feeding him on unripe fruit. So we conclude that what he says he likes he really does not like, and to please him therefore, it becomes necessary to give him what he professes to dislike. Ergo, I will read him to sleep with the seventeenth chapter, part forty-nine of the works of Niet-Zhe on the co-ordination of our æsthetic powers in respect to the relative delights of pleasure and pain.*

I will do my Aunt Jerusha the credit of saying at this point that her method of putting me to sleep was efficacious. I do not ever remember having retained consciousness past the third paragraph of her remedy for insomnia.

I tremble to think of what I should have become had this fauntleroy process of rearing been allowed to continue unchecked. There were prigs enough in our family already without afflicting the world with another, and it rejoices me to this day to recall that just as we were reaching the point when it was either an early and beautiful demise in the odor of sanctity as a perfect child, or my present eminence as the most continuous human performance on record for me, my father stepped in, reasserted his authority and rescued me from the clutches of my Aunt Jerusha. Returning one day from business, he discovered Aunt Jerusha sitting in a rocking-chair in the nursery before me reading aloud from her tablets, whilst I, as usual, hung strapped and suspended from a hook on the picture molding. It was my supper-time, and she was feeding me according to the New Thought method of catering. The substance of her discourse was that hunger was an idea, nothing more. She was proving to her own satisfaction at least that I was hungry only because I thought I was hungry, and as father came in she was trying to persuade me that if I would be a good boy and make up my mind that my appetite had been appeased by a series of courses of thought biscuits, spirituelle waffles, and mental hors d'œuvres generally I would no longer be hungry.

"Fill your spirit stomach with the food of thought, Methy, dear," she was saying as my father appeared in the door-way. "Make up your mind that it is stuffed with the crackers and milk of the spirit; that your spiritual bread is buttered with the oleomargerine of lofty ideals, and sugared with the saccharin of your granulated meditations, and you will grow strong. You will become an intellectual athlete, like the great King Ptush of Egypt; a winner in the spiritual Marathon –"

"What are you trying to do with this kid, anyhow?" demanded my father at this point. "Turn him into a strap-hanger, or is this just a little lynching party?"

"Hush, Enoch," protested Aunt Jerusha. "Do not project an unsympathetic thought wave across our wires. I am just getting little Methy into a receptive mood. He is having his supper."

"Supper?" roared my father. "You call that stuff supper? Why, the child is getting thinner than a circus lemonade –"

"In the grosser sense, yes," replied Aunt Jerusha, calmly, after the manner of maiden ladies who are sure of their position. "But look at those eyes. Do they not betoken a great and budding soul within that is hourly waxing in strength and beauty?"

"My dear Jerusha," said my father, unhooking me from the wall and handing me a ripe red banana to eat, "all that you say is very lovely, and I have no doubt that under your administration of affairs the boy will sooner or later become a bully idea, but I hate a man whose convexity of soul has been attained through a concavity of stomach. What this boy needs at this stage of the game is development in what you properly term the grosser sense, I might even go so far as to say the butcher sense as well as the grocer sense. Ham and eggs is what he needs."

And with that he sent out and had a diplodocus carnegii killed, and fed me himself for the next ten days on dainty morsels cut from the fatted calf of that luscious bird. It was thus that I escaped the fate of the overgood who die young and became a factor in the world of affairs rather than a pleasant memory in the minds of my family.

As for my education it was limited, and I may say desultory. In this my Aunt Jerusha was allowed a greater authority than in the matter of my diet, and she early made up her mind that the great weakness of the educational system of the day was the tendency of the teachers in our schools to cram the minds of the young.

"There is no hurry in days like these when people live to be eight or nine hundred years old," she observed to my mother. "There is not very much to be learned as yet. Science is in its infancy, very little history has been made, and as for Latin and Greek, it is entirely unnecessary for Methy to study those languages, because as yet, nobody speaks them, and with the possible exception of that tramp poet, Homer, who passed through here last week on his way West, nobody is using it in literature. Teach him the three Rs and all will be well. Taking the alphabet first and learning one letter a year for twenty-six years he will be able to read and write as early in life as he ought to. If we were more careful not to teach our children to read in their childhood we should not be so anxious about the effects of pernicious literature upon their adolescent morals. If I had my way no one should be taught to read until after he had passed his hundredth year. In that way, and in that way only can we protect our youth from the dreadful influence of such novels as 'Three Cycles, Not To Mention The Rug,' which dreadful book I have found within the past month in the hands of at least twenty children in the neighborhood, not one of whom was past sixty."

It was thus resolved that my education should proceed with due deliberation and even as Aunt Jerusha had suggested, I was taught only one letter a year for the first twenty-six years of my life, after which I took up addition, multiplication, short and long division and fractions. My father would not permit me to learn subtraction.

"It is a waste of time," said he. "Children subtract by intuition. Put in all your time teaching Methy how to add and multiply."

My history was meager, because as Aunt Jerusha had said, history itself was meager. There had not even been a flood, much less a first, second, or third Punic War. Nobody in my time had ever heard of Napoleon Bonaparte or George Washington or Julius Cæsar, or Alexander, save a few prophets in the hills back of Enochsville, in whose prognostications few of their contemporaries took any stock; as was indeed not unnatural, since when they attempted to prophesy as to the weather they showed themselves to be rather poor guessers. If a man prophesies a blizzard for tomorrow and tomorrow comes bringing with it the balmy odors of Spring, no one is likely to set much store by his prognostications concerning the possible presidential candidacy of a man named Bryan six or seven thousand years later. Consequently the only history with which I took the trouble to familiarize myself was that which ante-dated my birth, and even that was somewhat hazy in the minds of historians. My predecessors in the patriarchal profession were a reticent lot, inherited no doubt from our original ancestor Adam, who could never be got to talk even to members of his immediate family on the subject of his early years. True, it is generally believed that he had no early years, and that he was born on his fifty-ninth birthday, but even as to that he would not speak. I shall never forget the look on his face when I asked him at a Thanksgiving dinner one year if he had ever been a monkey with a tail. He rose up from the table with considerable dignity, and leading me out into the wood-shed turned me over on his knee and subjected me to a rather severe course of treatment with a hair-brush.

"There, my lad," he observed when he had done. "If I had had a tail that is about where I should have worn it."

I never referred to the subject again.

Chapter III

SOME REMINISCENCES OF ADAM

The concluding paragraphs of my last chapter have set my mind running upon the subject of my original forebears, and inasmuch as I have decided to write these memoirs of mine along the lines of least resistance, it becomes proper that I should at this time, put down whatever happens to be in my mind. To speak frankly I never really could get up much of a liking for old grandfather Adam. He was as devoid of real humor as the Scottentots, and simply because by a mere accident of birth he became the First Gentleman of Europe, Asia and Africa, he assumed airs that rendered him distinctly unpopular with his descendants. He considered himself the fount of all knowledge because in the early days of his occupancy of the Garden of Eden there was no one to dispute his conclusions, and the fact that he had been born without a boyhood, as we have already seen at the age of fifty-nine, left him entirely unsympathetic in matters where boys were concerned. I shall never forget a conspicuous case in point demonstrating his utter lack of comprehension of a boy's way of looking at things. He was on a visit to our home at Enochsville, and on the night of his arrival, having called for a glass of fermented grape-juice, thinking to indulge in a mere pleasantry, I brought him a tumblerful of sweetened red ink, the which he gulped down so avidly that it was not until it was beyond recall that he realized what I had done; and when in his wrath he called for an instant remedy and I brought him the blotting paper, instead of smiling at the merry quality of my jest, he pursued me for two hours around my father's farm, and finally cornering me in the Discosaurus shed, larruped me for twenty full minutes with a paddle pulled from a prickly cactus plant in my mother's drawing room, thorn side down. Indeed most of my early recollections of the old gentleman are inseparably associated with a series of chastisements which, even as he had prophesied when administering them, I have not been able to forget, although I cannot see that any of them ever resulted in a lasting reformation of my ways. On the contrary the desire to see what new form of thrashing his disciplinary mind could invent led me into devising new kinds of provocation, so that for a great many years his visits to our house were a source of great anxiety to my parents. His view of me and my ways were expressed with some degree of force to our family physician who, when at the age of a hundred and fifty-three I came down with the mumps, having summoned the whole family and said that I would burst before morning, was met by a reassuring observation from Adam that he wouldn't believe I was dead even if I had been buried a year.

"It is the good who die young, Doctor," he said. "On that principle this young malefactor will live to be the oldest man in the world."

A curious example of his gift of prophecy!

Adam's table manners were a frequent source of mortification to us all. The free and easy habits of the Garden period clung to him throughout his life, and under no circumstances could he be induced to use either a fork, a knife or a spoon, and even on the most formal occasions he absolutely refused to dress for dinner.

"Fingers were made before forks," he said, "and as for spoons I have no use for such frills. I can eat my peas out of the pod, and as for soup it tastes better out of a dipper anyhow."

As for the knives, his dislike of them was merely in their use at table. He was fond of knives of all sorts, and he regarded them always as his legitimate spoil whenever he dined anywhere, pocketing everyone he could lay his hands on with as much facility as the Egyptian, and Abyssinian drummers who visited our section of the country every year made off with the spoons of our hostelries. Nor could we ever appeal to him on the score of etiquette. Any observation as to the ways of our first families was always met by a cold but quick response that if there was any firster family than his own in all creation, he couldn't find its name in the social register. Indeed the old gentleman was rather inclined to be very snobbish on this point, and when any of his descendants chose to take him to task for the crudeness of his manners he was accustomed to look them coldly over and retort that things had come to a pretty pass when comparatively new people ventured to instruct the oldest of the old settlers as to what was or was not good form. The only person who ever succeeded in bowling him over on this point was Uncle Zib, hitherto referred to as the billionaire member of our family, who, after listening to a long and somewhat supercilious discourse from Adam on the subject of family, turned like a flash and asked:

"And who pray was your grandfather?"

The old gentleman flushed deeply, and for once was silent, being as I have already intimated rather sensitive, and therefore inclined to reticence on the score of his ancestry.

He took a great deal of pride in his success as a namer of animals, but as my grandson Noah remarked several hundred years later, it was a commonplace achievement after all.

"A dog is a dog, and a cat is a cat, and a horse is a horse. Any fool would know that, so what virtue there was in his calling the beasts by their real names I don't quite see," said Noah.

I am disposed, however, to give the old fellow the credit that is his due for making so few mistakes. That he should instantly be able to tell the difference between a dromedary and a camel without any previous instruction, strikes me as evidence of a more or less remarkable intuition, the like of which we do not often find today, and his dubbing that long-eared, four-footed piece of resistant uselessness the Ass an ass, always seemed to me to be a masterstroke, although my father used to say that his greatest achievement lay in correctly designating the pig at first sight.

"If there is any animal in the whole category of four-legged creatures that more thoroughly deserves to be called a pig than the pig, I don't know what it is. He looks like a pig, he behaves like a pig, and he eats like a pig – in fact he is a pig, and Adam never did anything better than when he invented that name and applied it."

The old gentleman was present when my father said that, and his face flushed with pleasure at his words of praise.

"Thank you, Enoch," he said. "I am rather proud of it, but I think I did quite as well when it came to the hen. Anything more aptly answering to the word hen in all its various shades of meaning than the hen itself I don't know, but it took me a full week to reason the thing out. It was not until I heard its absurd cackling over the laying of a strictly fresh egg, strutting about the barn-yard like a feathered Napoleon Bonaparte, and acting altogether as though she were the winner of a Twentieth Century Marathon race that it dawned on me that the creature was a hen, and could never be anything else than a hen. Mother wished me to call her an omelet, the feminine form of an om, as she expressed it, but I had already named the rooster, and the bird seemed so exactly like a rooster that I declined to make any changes."

"I don't see," put in Uncle Zib at this point, "where you got the word hen from. That is the wonder of it to my mind."

"Oh," laughed Adam, "that was easy, my dear Zib. I got it from an inspection of the egg."

"The egg?" demanded Uncle Zib.

"Certainly," replied Adam. "You see the minute I picked up the egg and looked at it closely, I saw that it was a hen's egg, and there you are."

After all it seemed very simple.

I have spoken of his abhorrence of dress. He carried this to an extreme degree and to the end of his life predicted dire things from the tendency of his descendants toward sartorial display. I shall never forget the lucid fashion in which he presented the situation to my father once while we were camping out one night on Mount Ararat, after a day's hunting. He was seated on a woody knoll skinning a pterodactyl for our supper.

"I tell you, Enoch," he said, "and if you don't mark my words you'll wish you had, these new fangled notions that are coming along, and affecting the whole of modern society in respect to what you are pleased to call dress, are going to result sooner or later in trouble. I can clearly see even if you cannot, that the new ideas as to clothes are breeders of extravagance. As things were in my young days anybody who felt the need of a new costume of one kind or another had only to go out into the woods and pick it. If your great-great-great-grandmother or I, for instance, wanted a new Spring suit we'd go hand in hand together to the orchard, and in the course of a half hour's steady work would fit ourselves out with a wardrobe that would have made this Queen of Sheba that the prophets are foretelling, look like thirty clam-shells; and what is more, a Spring costume was indeed a Spring costume and nothing else, for it was made of the freshest of the vernal leaves, beautiful in their early greens, and decorated here and there with a bit of a blossom that gave the whole a most fetching appearance. And so it was with the other seasons. For summer we used leaves of the vintage of July and August, deeper in their green, with the summer flowers for decoration. Nothing ever so stirred the heart of man as Mother Eve decked out in her gown of rose leaves, or hollyhocks; and occasionally when we went traveling together dressed in our suits of hardy perennials, we were the cynosure of all eyes. In the Autumn the rich red of the maple gave us an aspect of gayety in respect to our clothes that was most picturesque; and then when the winter blasts began to blow, our garments of pine, cedar and hemlock were not only warm, but appropriate and becoming. It is true that clothes made of hemlock were not altogether comfortable at first, having some of the prickly qualities of the hair-shirt, but the very titillation of the epidermis by their pointed spills, sharp sometimes as a needle, served to keep our blood in circulation, and consequently at all times warm and glowing. And it all cost us nothing more than the labor of the harvest, but now, all is different. The use of costly fabrics, woven stuffs, silks, satins and calicos, has introduced an added element of expense into our daily lives, and all to no useful purpose. Take your Aunt Jerusha, for instance. Where Mother Eve enjoyed as many different costumes as there were trees in the country without cost, all of them becoming, and wholly adequate, your Aunt Jerusha has to be satisfied with three or four gowns of indifferent fit, made by the village seamstress at an average cost of thirty or forty dollars apiece. A sheath-gown, costing Jerusha seventy-five dollars, in the distance, gives no more of an impression in the matter of figure to an admiring world than your original grandmother used to make without any further sartorial embellishment than an ostrich feather in her hair, and as for the men – well, if you see any value in the change in men's garments over those which prevailed in my day, you can see what I cannot, and what is going to be the result? The time will come when tailors' bills will be regarded as a curse. Fathers of families who, under the scheme of dress invented by myself, could keep a large number of growing boys appropriately clad, will sooner or later be forced into bankruptcy by the demands of tailors under these new methods now coming into vogue. In the train of this will come also a love of display, and in the course of years you will find men judged not by the natural stature of their manhood, but by the clothes they wear, to the everlasting deception of society. By the use of a little expert padding, building up here and there, a miserable little human shoat will be able to appear in all the glory of a gladiator. A silk outer garment will cover the shoddy inner nature of a bit of attleboro humanity so effectively that you will hardly be able to tell the real thing from the bogus, and many a man lured into matrimony by the charms of an outward Venus, will find after marriage that he has tied himself up for life to a human hat-rack, specially designed by a clever dressmaker, to yank him from the joys of a contented celibacy into the thorny paths of hymeneal chaos.

"Nor will it stop here," the old gentleman continued, warming to his subject. "I prophesy that just as at the present time society looks with disfavor on me for going around in the simple dress of my early days, so the time will come when an even more advanced society will demand the placing of more clothes on top of those that you all wear now. The outer garments of today will become the under-clothes of some destined tomorrow, and centuries hence a man found walking on the public highways dressed as you are will be arrested by the police for shocking the sense of propriety of the community, and so on. It will go on and on until you will find human beings everywhere decked out in layer after layer of clothes until he or she has lost all semblance to that beautiful thing that an all-wise Providence has designed us to be. Man will wear under-clothes and outer clothes. He will devise an absurd bit of starch, buttonholes and tails called a shirt, in which doubtless he will screw diamond-studs, and over which he will wear a resounding waistcoat embroidered with all sorts of wild-flowers in bloom. Then will come a stiff uncomfortable yoke for his neck, which he will call a collar, around which he will wind what he will call a necktie, the only useful purpose of which will be its value as a danger signal to the rest of mankind, for it will be through the medium of this addition to the human dress that character will manifest itself, man being prone unconsciously to show his strength or weaknesses in the manner of his personal adornment. This will lead to all sorts of vain exhibitions until it will be with extreme difficulty that the public will be able to differentiate between a genuine peacock and an upstart jack-daw, masquerading in a merry widow hat. Then will come the crowning misdemeanor in men's clothes which, for want of a better term let us call pants – a pair of bags sewed together at the top, and designed for no other purpose than to conceal from the world the character and quality of the wearer's legs. When that beatific invention arrives your spindle-legged, knock-kneed imitation of a man will, as far as the public eye is concerned, find himself on as sure a footing as your very Adonis, and a person with a comparatively under-developed understanding will be able to make as good a showing in the world as the man who is really all there. Like charity, these pants will cover a multitude of shins that once exposed to the world would at once give warning of the possessors' fundamental instability. In other words this new style of dress that our fashionable leaders are now advocating is designed simply for the purpose of concealing from the world their natural defects, enabling them to appear for what they are not, and therefore to deceive, the sure result of which is to be the fostering of vanity, a love of display, the breeding of snobs, and an impairment of the average man's purse to such an extent that some day or other tailors' and dressmakers' bills will become an inevitable item in every schedule in bankruptcy in the land. Clothes will also breed rags, for without clothes to grow threadbare and frayed, it is clear that the raw material of rags and tatters would be lacking, and many a scene of beggary would be avoided.

"Wherefore, my son," the old man concluded, "let me warn you to set your face sternly against these modern innovations, and to return to the plainer, and yet more beautiful habiliments of your sires. Let the sturdy oak be your tailor; when you need a vernal gown, seek the spreading chestnut tree and from its upper branches pluck the clothing that you need, and when drear winter comes upon the scene hie you to the mountain top, and from the rich stock of Hemlock, Pine and Co., Tailors, By Special Appointment To Their Majesties, The Eternal Hills, gather the sartorial blessings that there await you."

Chapter IV

GRANDMOTHER EVE

Very different in almost every imaginable respect from Adam was his attractive lady, Madame Eve. Indeed, so radically different from each other were this rather ill-assorted pair that it was always difficult for us to believe that they were related even by marriage, and I hesitate to say what I think would have been the outcome of their little romance had there been any competition for the lady's hand when Adam set out to win it. I have personally always had a feeling that this first of hymeneal experiments was rather a marriage of convenience than anything else, and I have heard my great-great-great-grandmother say that in the old pioneer days there was very little for a woman to choose from in the matter of men's society.

"For a long time," she remarked, "Adam was the only man in sight, and I was a young thing entirely without experience in worldly matters. He seemed to my girlish fancy to be all that a man should be. His habits were good. He neither smoked nor drank, cared apparently nothing for cards, and barring an interest in Discosaurus Racing, had very few sporting proclivities. We were thrown together a great deal, and inasmuch as the life in the Garden was a somewhat lonely one, we took considerable pleasure in each other's society. For myself, I was not particularly anxious to be married, preferring the free and independent life of the spinster, but as time went on and we came to realize that the people of future generations might misunderstand us and, as people will do, talk about us, we decided that the best way to avoid all gossip was to announce our engagement, and at the end of the usual period, settle down together as man and wife. I don't know that I have ever regretted the step, though I will say that I think it is undesirable for a young girl to enter too hastily into the obligations of matrimony, or to marry the first man that comes along, unless she is absolutely sure that he is the only man she could possibly endure through three meals a day for the balance of her life."

It must not be assumed from this little reminiscence of this first lady in the land that her marriage was an unhappy one. I think, that as a matter of fact, it was quite the contrary, for subsequent to the wedding each was too busy with other matters to get thinking either morbidly or otherwise on the subject of their individual happiness. They took it as a matter of course, and in the division of labor which the social conditions of the day involved, found too much to occupy them to worry over such unimportant abstractions as mere personal felicity.

"We were spared one of the direst afflictions of modern social life," Madame Eve once remarked to my mother, in talking over the old days, "in the absence of domestic servants from our family circle. Adam was head of the house, general provider, hired-man, stable boy, head-gardener, coach-man, night-watchman and everything else of the male persuasion on the place;

whilst I was cook, laundress, nurse, housekeeper, manicure, stenographer, and general housemaid, as well as the mother of the family – a situation that even though it involved us in no end of hard work, had its compensations. Living off in suburbs as we did, you can have no idea of what a comfort it was to us not to be at the mercy of a cook who would threaten to leave us every time anything happened to displease her, such as an extra meal to be cooked in emergency cases, or the failure of the cooking-sherry to come up to the exalted standards of her taste as a connoisseur in wines, and hard as the housework was, as I look back upon it now, I realize how much trouble I was spared in not having to follow a yellow-haired fluffy ruffles about the house all day long cleaning up after her. If there is anything of the labor-saving device in that modern invention known as a chambermaid, I don't know where it comes in. I'd rather sweep three floors, and make twenty-nine beds, every day of my life than put in one single week trying to get seven cents worth of efficient work out of a fourteen-dollar housemaid."

At this point I ventured to put in the suggestion that I should have thought some use could have been made of the monkeys in the matter of Domestic Service, whereupon the dear lady, who was not nearly so sensitive on the subject of the Simian family as her husband had always shown himself to be, patted me on the head, and smiled indulgently, as she cracked her little joke.

"Monkeys, my dear Methy," she replied, "were always more efficient in the higher branches. Seriously, however," she went on, "we had that same idea ourselves, and we tried Simian labor for a while, but it was far from satisfactory. They were too playfully impetuous, and we had to give them up as indoor servants. We had a Monkey Butler one season, and nothing could induce him to serve our dinner in that dignified fashion in which a dinner should be served. He would pass the soup with one paw, the fish with the other, while serving the bread with his tail, and all simultaneously, so that instead of dinner becoming a peaceful meal, it was at all times, a highly excitable function that left us all in a state of trembling nervousness when it was over. Try as we might we could not induce them to do one thing at a time, and finally when this particular butler, to whom I have referred, instead of standing as he was instructed to do behind Adam's chair, insisted on swinging from the chandelier over the center of the table suspended by his caudal appendage, we decided that we would rather wait on ourselves."

Asked once if she had not found the primitive life uncomfortable, she shook her head in a decided negative.

"There were too many compensations in our freedom from the things that make your social life of today a complex problem," she replied. "In the first place I never had to worry much over Adam. When he was not out getting the raw material for our daily meals he was most generally at home, for the very excellent reason that there was no other place to go. We hadn't any Clubs to begin with, so that on his way home from business there was no temptation for him to stop off anywhere and frivol away his time playing billiards, or squandering his limited means on rubbers of bridge or other ruinous games. The only Vaudeville shows we had at the time consisted of the somewhat too continuous performances of the monkeys and the poll-parrots right there in our own back-yard, so that that menace to the happy home was entirely unknown to us, and inasmuch as I was the only cook in all Christendom at the time, the idea of not coming home to dinner never occurred to Adam. It is true that at times he criticized my cooking, but in view of certain ancestral limitations from which he suffered, I never had to sit quietly and listen to an exasperating disquisition on the Pies That Mother Used To Make, a line of conversation that in these modern days has broken up many an otherwise happy home. Socially the time had its draw-backs, but even in that respect there were advantages. The fact that we had no next-door neighbors enabled us to live without ostentation. I have discovered that much of the trouble in the world today arises from a love of showing-off, and of course, if there is no one about to show-off to, you don't indulge in that sort of foolishness. Being the only family in the place we were not spurred into extravagances of living, either because we had to keep up an end in society, or because we wished to make a better showing than someone else was making. There was correspondingly no gossip going on all about us. The absence of society meant that there were no Sewing Circles anywhere where peoples' reputations were pulled apart while under-clothes for alleged heathen were put together. Nobody ever descended upon us at unreasonable hours with unwelcome Surprise Parties eating us out of house and home and compelling us to stay up all night dancing the Virginia Reel when we were so sleepy we could hardly keep our eyes open. We didn't have to give dinners to people we didn't like, or make calls on persons in whom we took no earthly interest whatever. There was no question of Woman's Suffrage to make an everlasting breach between Adam and myself; no church squabbles over whether the new carpet should be pink or green, and as for politics, there was not anything even remotely resembling a politic in the whole broad land. If Adam or I felt the need of a law now and then, we'd make it, and if it didn't work, we'd repeal it, so that there were no endless discussions on such subjects, involving hard feeling, acrimonious correspondence, and an endless chain of Chapters of the Ananias Club all over creation. And when the children came along I was permitted to bring them up according to my own ideas, thanks to the entire absence from the country of inspired old-maids, and omniscient editors, ceaselessly endeavoring to reduce a natural maternal function to an arbitrary science. It has been said that I did not have much to be proud of in the results of my efforts to bring up my children right, and I suppose that in the case of Cain and Abel I must admit that I have not; but I am not so sure that things would have turned out any different if I had reared them after a Fireside Companion pattern for the making of a panne velvet posterity. I will go so far as to say that after looking over the comic supplements of the Sunday Newspapers, I believe Cain would have killed Abel ten years earlier than he did if he had had the example of the Katzenjammer Kids and Buster Brown before him in the formative years of his life. So, on that score, I am comfortable in my mind, much as I regret the disastrous climax of the lives of those two boys. In connection with this matter of the bringing up of children I believe, too, that despite the narrowness of our outlook, the primitive conditions were better than those which now exist. I never heard of my boys running loose about town waking up the whole community with their cheers because their college football team had crippled eleven other boys from another college for life; and hard to manage as Cain and Abel were at times, Adam and I never had to put them to bed at five o'clock in the morning because they had paralyzed their throats at a college banquet announcing to an exasperated world that they were Sons of a Gambolier. In fact, the educational problem of those early days was an educational problem and not a social one. We did not spend our time teaching boys to speak seventeen languages, without any ideas to express in any one of them, but went in for the ideas first. We regarded speech merely as a vehicle for the expression of ideas, and went at it from that point of view, rather than the other way around according to modern notions. Cain and Abel didn't have to go to a military school to learn how to haze each other, and no young man of that day ever thought of qualifying for his A. B. by compelling another young man to sip Tabasco sauce through a straw. What they learned, they learned by experience, and not through the pages of a book. If we felt it well to teach one of them that water was wet, we did not subject his young mind to a nine months course of lectures by a Professor on Hydropathy, but took him out and dropped him in the duck-pond and let him draw his own conclusions; and when it came to Botany, we found that either one of them could get a more comprehensive idea of the habits of growing plants from weeding a ten-acre lot than he could get out of a four years' course at a Correspondence School. The result was that when he came to graduate and go out into the world he was ready for business, and didn't have to serve as an Office-Boy on a salary of nothing a week for seventy-five or a hundred years before he was able to earn his own living."

It surely was an idyllic picture that the dear old lady drew, and I have often wished myself amid the rush and roar of modern life, that we might go back to the simpler methods of those Arcadian days.

On the subject of dress, Eve was entirely out of accord with her husband. She viewed Adam's theories on that subject with toleration, however, and always laughed when they were mentioned.

"He's just like a man," she smiled. "He really has no objection to fetching costumes when they are worn by other people. He merely does not wish to be bothered with such things himself. He has just as much of an eye for a daintily dressed little bit of femininity as anybody else, but he is eternally afraid that if I go in for that sort of thing he will be turned into a lady's maid. The idea of a hook-and-eye fills him with horror. His eyesight is not as good as it used to be, and he dreads the notion that if I come out in one of these new-fangled waists that hook up at the back he will be compelled to put in an hour or two fastening it up for me every time I put it on, and I don't blame him. It seems to me that if there is anything in this world that is unbefitting the glorious manhood of a true masculine being it is to have to sit down in a chair for an hour before dinner looking for a half million hooks and eyes, or cloth-covered buttons and loops, on the back of his wife's gown, and trying to fasten them up properly without the use of language unsuited to a lady's ears. When you think that the hand of man was made to wield the scepter of imperial power over this magnificent world, it becomes a gross impropriety to divert it from the path of destiny into so futile an effort as hooking up a mere bit of fuss, feathers and fallals. You might just as well hitch up a pair of thoroughbred elephants to a milk wagon. It will do, as Adam says, for the Mollycoddle and the meticulous weakling, but never for a real man worthy of the name. But after all that is no reason why woman should be shorn of one of her chief glories, and I totally disagree with him in his condemnation of all clothes just because some of them are conceived in foolishness. Dresses can be made to button up at the side, or in front, and when I think of some of the new fall styles that are coming in I find myself regretting that I am over five hundred years old, and cannot with strict propriety, go in for them myself. Take those little chiffon –"

And so the dear old lady went on into an enthusiastic disquisition on the glories of dress that was so intimately feminine that I hesitate to attempt to quote her words in this place, knowing little as I do on the subject, and hardly able myself to tell the difference between a gimp and a café parfait. I will merely close this chapter by quoting Eve's last remark on the subject.

"All I can say is," she observed, "that Adam makes a great mistake in objecting to woman's thinking so much about her clothes, for I can tell him that if she didn't think about her own clothes she would begin to think about his, and if that were to happen it wouldn't be long before all men in creation would be going about looking as if somebody had picked them off a Christmas tree. In the matter of clothes woman is the court of last resort, and it is better for men that she should concentrate all her attention on herself!"

Incidentally let me add that when someone once asked Eve if she hadn't often wished she had been a man, she replied:

"Lord no! In that case there would have been two of us, and goodness knows one was enough!"

Chapter V

SOME NOTES ON CAIN AND ABEL

My acquaintance with my great-uncles, Cain and Abel, was not particularly intimate and in later years they are seldom spoken of by members of the family for reasons sufficiently obvious to need no mention here. Every family must sooner or later develop an undesirable or two, and on the whole I think that we have done tolerably well in having up to this time only one portrait in our Rogues' Gallery. Just what has become of Cain no one at this writing is aware, but wherever he is I hope when these memoirs of mine are published he will read them far enough to note that one member of the family at least holds him in pleasant recollection for the fun he has afforded him in the past. The two first boys of creation were not bad fellows at all, although as was natural, their bringing up resulted in a general condition of pure cussedness that at times became appalling to their parents. The fact that there had never been any other boys in the world before placed Adam and Eve at a considerable disadvantage in rearing these two youngsters. There were no precedents to go by, and as a consequence the lads were permitted to do a good many things that our modern boys would not dream of doing. There were no schools to send them to, and no Sunday Newspapers with Woman's Pages to instruct Eve in the Complete Science of Motherhood, so that when Cain and Abel came along to bless the world with their presence, neither their father nor their mother knew what on earth to do with them. Then, too, Eve's household duties were such that they very nearly absorbed all her time, and for years the youthful scions of this first family in the land were left to the tender mercies of a kindly old Gorilla who, however amiable and willing she may have been, was hardly the kind of person a modern mother would choose as an influence in the formative years of her children's development. I am quite aware that in some sections of the country today this old-time custom of leaving the young to the care of servants still prevails, and in some cases it has its distinct advantages considering the moral characteristics of the parents who so leave them, but as a social custom to be commended it is an entire failure, and was adopted by Eve not from choice, but from necessity. It was not through any desire to shine in society as a constant attendant at the Five o'Clock teas of her time, or, because she deemed that her duty lay in trying to secure the alleged Emancipation of her Sex from imaginary shackles at the expense of her home life and its responsibilities; or, because she believed that the primary duty of a mother was to provide her offspring with a maternal relative who could expound the most abstruse philosophies of the age with her eyes shut, that led Mother Eve into an apparent neglect of her children. It was simply the inevitable result of the life of her time. One can hardly be all that she had to be whether she wanted to be it or not and at the same time fulfill all the functions of motherhood. The daily labors of a large ranch such as the world practically was at that time were of enormous proportions, and with all due respect to Adam it has always been my profound belief that a good ninety percent of them were performed by Eve. It was she who had to look after the domestic details of the hour, day in and day out, while he after the fashion of mankind, led the freer life of the open. Indeed I have never found that in the matter of manual labor Adam was in any wise noted. The naming of the animals was a purely intellectual achievement, and while, of course, he was the provider when it came to getting in the food supply, I have never observed that any man yet created ever regarded a day on a trout stream with a fly and a rod, or a chase through the forest after a venison steak, or a partridge, as in any way even remotely resembling work. On the contrary Adam lived the life of a Naturalist and a Nimrod, while Eve faithfully did the chores. It was inevitable then that the children when they first came along, should be allowed to grow wild, to associate with their inferiors, and to become confirmed in habits that were deplorable and reprehensible. I am entering upon no defense of my Uncle Cain. I do not excuse his misbehavior in the least, but when a censorious world holds up its hands in holy horror whenever he is mentioned, and uses his name as a synonym for evil, I would merely beg it to remember the lad's bringing up, and to ask itself whether under similar conditions it would do much better itself. Particularly do I ask that branch of human society, now growing rather larger than I like to see it, who are themselves allowing their children to grow up, not only removed but far away from all parental influences whatsoever, if they realize that they will have only themselves to blame if they add to the stock of unfortunates who bear the mark of Cain? Of course, a woman who would rather play Bridge than rock her baby to sleep would be a bad influence upon a budding soul at any time, and her child is to be congratulated when its mother's engagement card is full from Sunday to Sunday, but even a mother of that sort owes it to society to see that her place is filled not by any old gorilla from the handiest intelligence office that comes along as poor Eve was forced into doing, but by some capable person in whom the love of motherhood rules as strong as does the passion for the grand-slam in her own breast.

But enough of this moralizing! I had not meant to preach a sermon, and it is only because I see so many wistful little faces of motherless youngsters around me day after day – Social Orphans, whose mothers have not gone to Heaven, but to Mrs. Grundy's; children who with the qualities of service in their souls are treading dangerously near to the footsteps of the original scapegrace for lack of attention; that I have been led into this garrulous homily. It must not be supposed, either from what I have said that there was never any discipline in the Home of Adam and Eve. Later on there came to be a lot of it, and I am not sure that its excesses in later periods were not as evil in their influence as its utter lack at a time when ten minutes with the hair-brush would have done Cain more good than ten years in the county jail.

To the world at large these two boys are interesting because of the fact that they introduced humor into the world. Adam never had any, and Eve, as we have seen, was rather too busy to joke, but not so with the youngsters, who, doubtless from their constant association with the monkeys bubbled over with a kind of fun that though necessarily primitive, was quite appealing. It was Cain who invented that immortal riddle, "When is a door not a door?" the true answer being, "when it is a bird." This is as far as I have been able to discover the first thing in the nature of a joke ever known on this planet, though whether it was the one that made the original Hyena laugh I have not been able to ascertain. It is a joke that has appeared in modified form many times since. Even that illustrious pundit, Senator Chauncey M. DeMagog uses it as his most effective peroration at this season's public banquets. I heard him myself get it off at The Egyptian Society Dinner last month, as well as at the Annual Banquet of The Sons and Daughters of the Pre-Adamite Evolution, the month before, changing the answer, however, to "when it's a jar" – which I personally do not consider an improvement, for when a door becomes a jar I must confess I cannot see. A jar, as I understand it, is a vessel, a receptacle, a jug, a sort of demijohn, or decanter that people use to store up water, or to keep the juice of the grape in, like a pitcher, or an amphora; and how by any stretch of the imagination a door could become such a thing is beyond my ken, although I must say that the jest when told by the Senator in his own inimitable way, was received with shouts of laughter every time he got it off. For my own part I think that Cain's version is infinitely more humorous and instructive as well, because a "door is not a door" when it is a "daw," which is, indeed, as Cain's answer to the riddle claims it to be, a bird. It is, of course, a great compliment to Cain that the Senator and a hundred others I might name like him should go back to him for their humor, but I think they would do better if they took his jests exactly as they found them instead of trying to improve them to their destruction.

I find also in our family records that it was Abel who first asked the question, "Why is an elephant like an oyster? Because it cannot climb a tree," a jest that similarly to Cain's riddle, possesses not only true humor but is at the same time educational, as the best humor must always be, in that it teaches the young certain indubitable facts in the Science of Natural History, viz., that neither the pachyderm nor the bivalve, in common with several other carnivorous botanical specimens, is gifted similarly to the squirrel, the ant, or the grizzly bear.

Mother Eve, who always took a naïve delight in the droll sayings of her offspring, used to tell with great glee of Cain's persistent habit of asking questions of his father, some of which used to tax all the old gentleman's powers of invention to answer intelligently. One of these that I recall most vividly was as follows:

"Say, Pa," said Cain, one Saturday afternoon, when the whole family were off on a picnic together, "did you have any sisters?"

"No, my son," replied Adam, plucking a bottle of olives from a neighboring tree, and placing them on the outspread tablecloth on the grass.

"Well, did Ma have any sisters?" persisted Cain.

"No," said Adam. "Your mother had no sisters, either. Why do you ask?"

"Oh, nothin'," replied the lad with a puzzled expression coming over his face as he scratched his back. "I was just wonderin' where the Ants came from."

It was Abel on the other hand who asked his father why he had not named the male ants uncles, a question that to this day has not been satisfactorily answered. Indeed I have frequently found myself regretting that there was nobody at hand to ask Adam these very pertinent questions earlier in his life, and before it was too late to instill in his mind the idea that a little more consistency would be desirable in his selection of names for the creatures he was called upon to christen. Zoölogy might have been a far simpler science in the matter of nomenclature than it is now ever likely to become, had Adam been surrounded at the beginning with inquiring minds like those of Cain and Abel, not necessarily to dispute his conclusions or his judgments, but to seek explanations. Why, for instance, should a creature that is found chiefly on the Nile, and never under any circumstances on the Rhine, be called a Rhinoceros? And why should a Caribou be called a Caribou entirely irrespective of its sex? There are Caribou of both sexes, when we might have had Caribou for one and Billibou for the other, and yet Adam has feminized the whole Bou family with no apparent thought about the matter at all. Then there is the animal which he called the Bear. He is not bare at all – on the contrary he wears the shaggiest coat of all the animals, except possibly the Buffalo, who, by the way, is not buff, but a rather dirty dull brownish black in color. The Panther does not wear pants, and the Monkey far from suggesting the habits of a Monk is a roistering, philanderous old rounder that would disgrace a heathen temple, much less adorn a Monastery. And finally if there is anything lower than a Hyena, or less coy than a Coyote, I don't know what it is.

There is considerable evidence in Mother Eve's Garden Book, in which she jotted down now and then little notes of her daily life that most of these points, or at least similar ones, were brought to Adam's attention at one time or another by his sons, and not always in a way that was pleasing to him. Indeed, as we read these notes we observe a growing tendency on Adam's part to be irritated by the enquiries which seem to have formed an inevitable part of the family conversation. At random I select the following:

August 3rd, 5569. Cain spanked and put to bed without his supper for asking his father why he had not called the male Kangaroo a Kangarooster.

September 5th, 5567. Cain sentenced to the wood-pile for four hours for enquiring of Adam why he called the Yak a Yak when everybody knew he looked more like a Yap. Adam is getting very nervous under this persistent questioning.

January 4th, 5565. Adam has just retired to the woodshed with poor Abel on what he termed a "whaling-expedition," to explain why he had named the elephant of the sea a whale instead of a sealephant. I judge from Abel's blubbering that his father is giving him an object lesson in the place where it is most likely to impress itself forcibly on his understanding, though I must say I think the child's idea a rather good one, and I often wish my dear husband would not be so sensitive on the subject of his possible mistakes.

May 25th, 5563. Adam has forbidden the children to ask anymore questions about the names of the animals, Cain having exasperated him by asking how much a guinea was worth.

"About five dollars," said Adam.

"Gee!" cried Cain. "You must have got stung on the guinea-pigs, then. They're dear at a dollar a dozen."

It may interest modern readers who seem to have created a demand for what is known as the Mother-in-Law joke that this style of humor found its origin in an early remark of Abel's, if his mother's Diary is to be believed. A visitor once interrupted him in the midst of a ball game that he was playing with Cain and a number of his Simian friends, to ask him how his grandmother was.

"Never had one," replied Abel, with a grin.

"Poor boy," sympathized the visitor. "And don't you wish you had?"

"Yes," said Abel. "I think a Mother-in-Law around the house would have done Pa good!"

I will close my remarks concerning these famous boys with a little poem which their mother had clipped from an Egyptian paper and pasted in her book. It seems to me to be a pretty accurate picture of two very interesting figures in our family history.

I don't suppose that Cain and Abel
Were very mannerly at table.
From what I've read by those that knew 'em
They'd speak when none had spoken to 'em,
And in a manner unbefittin'
Upon their shoulders they'd be sittin',
And sundry dinosaurs be treating
With scraps the while themselves were eating.
I fear they smacked their lips while pickin'
The bones of tarpon and spring chicken,
And each the other would be hazin'
To see who got the final raisin.
The notion in my brain-pan lingers
They ate their flapjacks with their fingers –
Not that their mother fair assented,
But knives and forks were not invented.
When there was pie, I fear they grabbed it,
Unless their Pa'd already nabbed it;
And that in fashion most unmoral
O'er cakes and puddings they would quarrel.
I don't believe that either chapkin
E'er thought at lunch to fold his napkin,
And if one biscuit graced the platter

'Twas ever less than fighting matter,
Or if they'd beans – no doubt they had 'em –
They failed to snap a few at Adam.
I fear me as they ate their salade
They hummed some raw primeval ballad,
And when the Serpent came to dinner,
They made remarks about the sinner.
No doubt they criticized the cooking
And hooked the fruit when none was looking,
And when they'd soup – O my! O Deary!
The very notion makes me weary.
About these youngsters let's stop writing
And turn to subjects more inviting!

I have never been able to ascertain the authorship of this poem, but if the poet ever sees this I hope he will be glad to know that I heartily agree with Mother Eve's memorandum written underneath the clipping in her book,

"I guess this scribe has had boys of his own!"

Chapter VI

HE CONFESSES TO BEING A POET

I do not know whether it is a part of the program mapped out for me that I am to live forever or not, and I realize the danger that a man runs in writing his memoirs if he put aught down in them which shall savor of confession. They say that confession is good for the soul, but I have not yet discovered anybody who was profited by it to any material extent. On the contrary, even the virtuous have suffered from it, as witness the case of my dear old Uncle Zekel. In his extreme youth Zekel went out one summer's day, the call of the wild proving too much for his boyish spirit, and ere night fell had done a certain amount of mischief, although intrinsically he came nearer to being a perfect child than anyone yet known to the history of the human race. Thoughtlessly the lad had chopped down one of his father's favorite date trees, the which when his father observed it, caused considerable consternation.

"Who did this thing?" he cried angrily, summoning the whole family to the orchard.

"Father," said Zekel, stepping forward, pale, but courageous, "I cannot tell a lie, I did it with my little tomahawk."

"Very well, my son," said the old gentleman, pulling a switch from the fallen tree, and seizing Zekel by the collar, "in order to impress this date more vividly upon your mind, we will retire to the barn and indulge in a little palmistry."

Whereupon he withdrew with Zekel from the public gaze and administered such a rebuke to the boy that forever afterwards the mere association of ideas made it impossible for Zekel to sit under a palm tree with any degree of comfort.*

I realize, however, that in writing one's memoirs one should not withhold the truth if there is to be any justification in the eyes of posterity for their existence, so I am not going to conceal anything from my readers that has any important bearing upon my character. Let me therefore admit here and now, apropos of the charming lines with which my last chapter was brought to a close, that I have myself at times written poetry. It is the lamentable fact that in this day and generation poets are not held in that high esteem which is their due. We have unfortunately had a number of them in this vicinity of late years who have not been any too particular about paying their board bills, and whether their troth has been plighted to our confiding maidens, or to our trustful tailors, the result has been the same – they have not been conspicuously present at the date of maturity of their promises. One very distinguished looking old gentleman in particular, who registered from Greece, came here several centuries ago and se-

---

* Editor's Note: It is very interesting to find this story in the Memoirs of Methuselah owing to its marked resemblance to an anecdote related of General Washington, in which the youthful father of his country is represented as having acted in a like manner upon a later occasion.

cured five hundred subscriptions to his book of verses, collected the first installment, and then faded from the scene and neither he nor his verses have been heard from since. The consequence has been that when any of the young of this community show the slightest signs of poetic genius their parents behave as though the measles had broken out in the family, and do all they can spiritually and physically to stamp out the symptoms. My cousin Aminidab indeed went so far while he was in the Legislature here, to introduce a bill making the writing of poetry a misdemeanor, and ordering the police immediately to arrest all persons caught giving way in public or private to an inspiration. The bill only failed to become a law by the expiration of the session before it had reached its final reading. It may be readily imagined, therefore, why until this I have never acknowledged my own proneness to expressing myself in verse. Only two or three of my most intimate friends have been aware of the tendency, and they have been so ashamed of it that as my friends they have sought rather to suppress than to spread the report.

I quite remember the consternation with which my first effort was received in the family. Father Adam had been reminiscing about the Garden Days, and he had made the remark that when some of the animals came up to be christened they were such extraordinary looking creatures he was afraid they were imaginary.

"Take the Ornithorhyncus, for instance," he said, "and the Discosaurus Carnegii – why, when they came ambling up for their tickets I could hardly believe my eyes, and I turned to Eve and asked her with real anxiety, whether or not she saw anything, and, of course, her answer reassured me, but for a minute I was afraid that the grape-juice we had had for lunch was up to its old tricks."

This anecdote amused me tremendously, for I had myself thought the Discosaurus about the funniest looking beast except the shad, I had ever seen, and I promptly constructed a limerick which I handed over to my father. It ran this way:

There was an old fellow named Adam,
Who lived in the Garden with Madam.
  When the critters they came
  All demanding a name
He thought for a minute he "had 'em!"

I don't think I shall ever forget the result of my father's horrified reading of the lines. All my grandfathers back to Adam himself were there, and wrath, fear, and consternation were depicted on every countenance when the last line was delivered, and then every eye was turned on me. If there had been any way of disappearing I should have faded away instantly, but alas, every avenue of escape was closed, and before I left the room each separate and distinct ancestor had turned me over his knee and lambasted me to his heart's content. In spite of all this discipline, which one would have thought effective enough to take me out of the lists of Parnassus forever, it on the contrary served only to whet my thirst for writing, and from that time until now I have never gotten over my desire to chisel out sonnets, triolets, rondeaux, and lyrics of one kind or another.

One little piece that I recall had to do with the frequency with which I was punished for small delinquencies. It was called

WHEN FATHER SPANKED ME

My Father larruped me, and yet
I could but note his eyes were wet,

When lying there across his knee
I got what he had had for me –
It seemed to fill him with regret.

"It hurt me worse than you," he said,
When later on I went to bed,
And I – the truth would not be hid –
Replied, "I'm gug-gug-glad it did!"

There were other verses written as I grew older that, while I do not regard them as masterpieces, I nevertheless think compare favorably with a great deal of the alleged poetry that has crept into print of late years. A trifle dashed off on a brick with a piece of charcoal one morning shortly after my hundredth birthday, comes back to me. The original I regret to say was lost through the careless act of one of my cousins, who flung it at a pterodactyl as it winged its flight across our meadows some years after. I reproduce it from memory.

THE JUNE-BUG

The merry, merry June-bug
Now butts at all in sight.
He butts the wall o' mornings,
He rams the ceil at night.

He caroms from the bookcase
Off to the windowpane,
Then bounces from my table
Back to the case again.

He whacks against the door-jamb
And tumbles on the mat;
Then on the grand-piano
He strikes a strident flat;

Then to the oaken staircase
He blindly flops and jumps,
And on the steps for hours
He blithely bumps the bumps.

They say that he is foolish,
And has no brains. No doubt
'Tis well for if he had 'em
He'd surely butt them out.

As I say, this is mere a trifle, but it is nonetheless beautifully descriptive of a creature that has always seemed to me to be worthy of more attention than he has ever received from the poets of our age. I have been unable to find in the literature of Greece, Egypt or the Orient, any reference to this wonderful insect who embodies in his frail physique so much of the truest philosophy of life, and who, despite the obstacles that seem so persistently to obstruct his path, buzzes blithely ever onward, singing his lovely song and uttering no complaints.

In the line of what I may call calendar poetry, which has always been popular since the art of rhyming began, none of the months escaped my attention, but of all of my efforts in that direction I never wrote anything that excelled in descriptive beauty my

ODE TO FEBRUARY

Hail to thee, O Februeer!
It is sweet to have you here,
Lemon-time of all the year!
Making all our noses gay
With the influenziay;
Flinging sneezes here and yon,
Rich and poor alike upon;

Clogging up the bronchial tubes
Of the Urbans and the Roobs;
Opening for all your grip
With its lavish stores of pip;
Scattering along your route
Little gifts of Epizoot;
Time of slush and time of thaw,
Time of hours mild and raw;
Blowing cold and blowing hot;
Stable as a Hottentot;
Coaxing flowers from the close
Just to nip them on the nose;
Calling birdies from their nests
For to freeze their little chests;
Springtime in the morning bright,
With a blizzard on at night;
Chills and fever through the day
Like a sort of pousse café;
Time of drift and time of slosh!
Season of the ripe golosh;
Running rivers in the street,
Frozen toes, and soaking feet;
Take this wreath of Poesie
Dedicated unto thee,
Undiluted stream of mush
To the Merry Month of Slush!

I preferred always, of course, to be original, not only in the matter of my thought, but in the manner of my expression as well, but like all the rest of the poetizing tribe, I sooner or later came under the Greek influence. This is shown most notably in a little bit written one very warm day in midsummer, back in my 278th year. It was entitled

TO PAN IN AUGUST

I don't wish to flout you, Pan.
Tried to write about you, Pan.
Tried to tell the story, Pan,
Of your wondrous glory, Pan;
But I can't begin it, Pan,
For this very minute, Pan,
All my thoughts are tumid, Pan,
'Tis so hot and humid, Pan,
And for all my trying, Pan,
There is no denying, Pan,
I can't think, poor sighing Pan,
Of you save as frying, Pan.

It was after reading the above, when it dropped out of my coat pocket during one of our visits to the wood-shed, that Adam expressed the profound conviction that I was born to be hanged, but as I have already intimated, neither his sense of justice, nor his sense of humor was notable.

Once in awhile I tried a bit of satire, and when my son Noah first began to show signs of mental aberration on the subject of a probable flood that would sweep everything before it, and put the whole world out of business save those who would take shares in his International Marine and Zoo Flotation Company, I endeavored to dissuade him in every possible way from so suspicious an enterprise. Failing to impress my feelings upon him in one way, I fell back upon an anonymously published poem, which I hoped would bring him to his senses. The lines were printed in red chalk on the board fence surrounding his Ship-Yard, and ran as follows:

MARINE ADVICES

O Noah he built himself a boat,
  And filled it full of animiles.
He took along a billie-goat,
  A pug and two old crocodiles.

A pair of very handsome yaks
  A leopard and hyenas two;
A brace of tender canvas-backs,
  A camel and a kangaroo.

A pair of guinea-pigs were placed
  In state-rooms off the main saloon,
Along with several rabbits chaste,
  A 'possum and a grey raccoon.

Now all went well upon that cruise,
  And they were happy as could be,
Until one morning came the news
  That filled old Noah with misery.

Those guinea-pigs – O what a tide! –
  Were versed in plain Arithmetic;
The way they upped and multiplied
  Made Captain Noah mighty sick.

And four days out he turned about,
  And made back to the pier once more
To rid himself of all that rout,
  And put the guinea-pigs ashore.

And where there were but two of these
  When starting on that famous trip,
When they got back from off the seas,
  Three hundred thousand left the ship!

Poor Noah! He took this publication so much to heart that he offered a reward of a thousand dollars, and a first-class passage on his cruise to the top of Mount Ararat to anyone who could give him the name of the miscreant who had written the lines, but he has never yet found out who did them, and until he reads these memoirs after I have passed away, he will never know from how near home they came.

Finally let me say that in a more serious vein as a Poet I was not wanting in success – that is in my own judgment. As a mystic poet nothing better than the following came from my pen:

O arching trees that mark the zenith hour,
How great thy reach, how marvelous thy power,
So lavishly outpouring all thy rotund gifts
On mortal ways, in superhuman shifts
That overtax the mind, and vex the soul of man,
As would the details of some awful plan,
Jocund, mysterious, complex, and yet withal
Enmeshed with Joy and Sorrow, as a pall
Envelops all the seas at eventide, and brings
New meaning to the song the Robin sings
When from her nest matutinal she squirms
And hies her forth for adolescent worms
With which her young to feed, yet all the time
With heart and soul laments my dulcet rhyme!

Of this I was naturally quite proud, and when under the title of "Maternity" I read it once in secret to my Aunt Jerusha, she burst into tears as I went on, and three days later read it as a New Thought gem before the Enochsville Society of Ethical Culture. It was there pronounced a great piece of symbolic imagery, and prediction was made that some day in some more advanced age than our own, a Magazine would be found somewhere that would print it. This may be so, but I fear I shall not live to see it.

Chapter VII

THE INTERNATIONAL MARINE AND ZOO FLOTATION COMPANY

I have never yet been quite able to make up my mind with any degree of definiteness in regard to the sanity of my son Noah. In many respects he is a fine fellow. His moral character is beyond reproach, and I have never caught him in any kind of a willful deception such as many parents bewail in their offspring, and I know that he has no bad habits. He has no liking for cigarette smoking, and he keeps good company and good hours. His sons Shem, Ham and Japhet, are great favorites with all of us, and as far as mere respectability goes there is no family in the land that stands higher than his, but the complete obsession of his mind by this International Marine and Zoo Flotation Company of his is entirely beyond my comprehension, and his attempts to explain it to me are futile, because its utter impracticability, and the reasons advanced for its use seem so absurd that I lose my temper before he gets halfway through the first page of his prospectus. From his boyhood up he has been fond of the water, and when the bath-tub was first invented we did not have to drive him to it, as most parents have to do with most boys, but on the contrary we had all we could do to keep him away from it. I don't think anyone in my household for five hundred years was able to take a bath on any night of the week without first having to clear away from the tub the evidence of Noah's interest in marine matters. Nothing in the world seemed to delight his spirit more as a child than to fill the tub full of water, turn on the shower at its fullest speed, and play what he called flood in it, with a shingle or a chip, or if he could not find either of these, with a floating leaf. Many a time I have found him long after he was supposed to have gone to bed sitting on the bathroom floor singing a roisterous nautical song like "Rocked in the Cradle of the Deep," or "A Life On the Ocean Wave," while he pushed a floating soap dish filled with ants, spiders and lady-bugs up and down that overflowing tub; and later in his life, when more manly sports would seem to be more to anyone's tastes, while his playmates were out in the open chasing the Discosaurus over the hills, or trapping Pterodactyls in the bull-rushes, he would go off by himself into the woods where he had erected what he called his ship-yard, and whittle out gondolas, canoes, battle-ships, arks and other marine craft day in and day out until one could hardly walk in the dark without stubbing his toe on some kind of a boat. I recall once coming upon him on the farther slopes of Mount Ararat, putting the finishing touches to as graceful a cat-boat as anyone ever saw – a thing that would have excited the envy of mariners in all parts of the world, but in spite of my admiration for his handicraft, it worried me more than I can say when I thought of all the labor he had expended on such a work miles away from any kind of a water course. It did not seem to square with my ideas as to what constituted sense.

"It is very beautiful, my son," I observed, after inspecting the vessel carefully for a few moments. "Her lines are perfect, and the model indicates that she will prove a speedy proposition, but it seems to me that you have left out one of the most important features of a permanently successful sailing vessel."

Noah looked at me patronizingly, and shrugged his shoulders as much as to inquire what on earth I knew about boat-building.

"If you refer either to the bowsprit or to the flying balloon-jib," he replied coldly, and acting generally as if he were very much bored, "you are entirely wrong. This isn't a sloop, or a catamaran, or a caravel. Neither is it a government transport, an ocean grey-hound, or a ram. It's just a cat-boat, nothing more."

"No," said I. "I refer to nothing of the sort. I don't know much about boats, but I know enough to be aware without your telling me, that this affair is not a battle-ship, tug, collier, brig, lugger, barge or gravy-boat. Neither is it a dhow, gig or skiff. But that does not affect the validity of my criticism that you have forgotten an important factor in her successful use as a sailing craft."

"What is it?" he demanded, curtly.

"An ocean," said I. "How the dickens do you expect to sail a boat like that off here in the woods, where there isn't enough water to float a parlor-match?"

He laughed quietly as I advanced this objection, and for the first time in his life gave evidence of the haunting idea that later took complete possession of his mind.

"Time enough for that," said he. "There'll be more ocean around here some day than you can keep off with a million umbrellas, and don't you forget it."

Somehow or other his reply irritated me. The idea seemed so preposterously absurd. How on earth he ever expected to get an ocean out there, halfway up the summit of our highest mountain, no sane person could imagine, and I turned the vials of my wrathful satire upon him.

"You ought to start a Ferry Company from the Desert of Sahara to the top of Mount Ararat," I observed, as dryly as I knew how.

"The notion is not new," he replied instantly. "I have already given the matter some thought, and it isn't impossible that the thing will be done before I get through. There will be a demand for such a thing all right some day, but whether it will be a permanent demand is the question."

It may interest the public to know that it was at this period that I invented a term that has since crept into the language as a permanent figure of speech. Speaking to my wife on the subject of the day's adventure that very evening, after I had expressed my determination to apply for the appointment of a Commission De Lunatico Enquirendo on Noah's behalf, she endeavored to quiet my anxiety on the score of his good sense by saying:

"Don't worry, dear. He is very serious in this matter. He has always had a great storm in his mind ever since he was a baby."

"I guess it's a brain-storm," I interjected contemptuously, for I could not then, and I cannot now conceive of any kind of a shower that will make the boy's habit of building caravels in the middle of ten-acre lots, and submarines on fifteen-by-twenty fishponds, and schooner yachts on mill-dams only three feet deep at high tide a reasonable bit of procedure.

Occasionally one of my neighbors would call upon me to remark somewhat critically on this strange predilection of my son, and several of them advised me to take the matter seriously in hand before it was too late.

"If you lived on the seaboard, it would be a fine thing to have such a son," they said, "but off here in the lumber district it would be far more to the point if he went in for the breeding of camels, or some other useful vehicle of transportation, instead of constructing ferry-boats that never can be launched, and building arks in a spot where the nearest approach to an ocean is a leak in the horse-trough."

I could not but admit that there was justice in these criticisms, but when it came to the point I never felt that I could justify myself in interfering with the boy's hobby until it was too late, and the lad having passed his three hundredth birthday, was no longer subject to parental discipline. I reasoned it out that after all it was better that he should be building dories and canal-boats out under the apple trees, and having what he called "a caulking good time," in an innocent way, than spending his time running up and down the Great White Way, between supper-time and breakfast, making night hideous with riotous songs, as many youths of his own age were doing; and when our family physician once tried to get him to join a football eleven at the Enochsville High School in order to get this obsession of a deluge out of his mind, I was not a little impressed by the impertinent pertinence of his ready answer.

"No rush-line for mine, Doctor," he said, firmly. "I'd rather have water on the brain than on the knee."

I had hoped that as the years passed on he would outgrow not only his conviction of the imminence of a disastrous deluge by which the world would be overwhelmed, and the predilection for nautical construction that the belief had bred in him, but alas for all human expectation, it grew upon him, instead of waning, as I had hoped. Our prosperous farm was given over entirely to the demands of his ship-yard, and when his sons, Shem, Ham and Japhet came along he directed all their education along lines of seamanship. He fed them even in their tender years upon hard-tack and grog. Up to the time when they were two hundred years old he made them sleep in their cradles, which he kept rocking continuously so that they would get used to the motion, and would be able to go to sea when the time came without suffering from sea-sickness. All clocks were thrust bodily out of his house, and if anybody ever stopped at the farm to inquire the time of day he was informed that it was "twenty minutes past six bells," or "nineteen minutes of three bells," or some other unmeaning balderdash according to the position of the sun. When the farmhouse needed painting, instead of renewing the soft and lovely white that had made it a grateful sight to the eye for centuries, Noah had it covered with pitch from roof to cellar, until the whole neighborhood began to smell like a tar barrel. And then he began his work upon this precious ark of his – Noah's Folly, the neighbors called it; placed in the middle of our old cow-pasture, twenty-five miles from the sea; about as big as a summer hotel, and filled with stalls instead of state-rooms! He mortgaged the farm to pay the first installment on it, and when I asked him how on earth he ever expected to liquidate the indebtedness he smilingly replied that the deluge would take care of everything that stood in need of liquidation when the date of maturity came round. He was even flippant on the subject.

"Don't talk about falling dew," he remarked. "There'll be something dewing around here before many days that will make you landlubbers wish your rubbers were eight or nine million sizes larger than the ones you bought last February; and as for liquidation – well, father dear, you can take my word for it that when this mortgage of mine is presented at my office for payment by its present holder there will be liquid enough around to float a new bond issue in case I can't pay in spot cash. If that is not satisfactory to my creditors, you still need not worry. I have a definite fund in mind that will take care of them."

"That is a relief," said I, innocently. "But may I ask what fund you refer to?"

"Certainly, father dear," he replied. "I refer to the Sinking Fund which will be in full working order the minute the deluge arrives."

This was about all the satisfaction I was ever able to get out of my son on the subject of his Ark, and after two or three hundred years I stopped arguing with him on the futile extravagance of his course. As we have seen in the last chapter of my memoirs, I did write a bit of verse on the subject which made him very angry, but beyond that I did nothing, and then the great scandal came!

It was the blackest hour of my life when it came to be rumored in and about Enochsville that Noah, now grown to independent estate, had method in his madness, and was about to embark upon a questionable financial enterprise. One of the yellow journals of the day – for we had them even then, although they were not put forth from printing presses, but displayed on board fences in scare-head letters six or eight feet high – one of the yellow journals of the day, I say, issued a muck-raking Extra, exposing what it termed *The International Marine and Zoo Flotation Company,* and most unfortunately there was just enough truth in the story in so far as its details went, to lend color to its sensational accusations. It could not be denied, as was stated in *The Enochsville Evening Gad,* that Noah had built a large, unwieldy vessel of his own designing in the old pasture up back of our Enochsville farm, miles away from tide-level. That it resembled what *The Gad* called a cross between a cow-barn and a Lehigh Valley Coal-Barge, was evident to anybody who had merely glanced at it. But what was its apparent purpose? asked the reporter of *The Gad.* Stated to be the housing of a menagerie during a projected cruise of forty-odd days! "What philanthropy!" ejaculated the editor of *The Gad.* What a kindly old soul was the projector of this wonderful enterprise, that he should take a couple of tired old elephants off on a Mediterranean trip out of the sheer kindness of his heart! Was it not the acme of generosity for a man who had lately been so hard up that he had mortgaged his farm to go to the expense of building a huge floating barge on which the gorillas, giraffes, and rhinoceri of the land, having lately shown signs of enfeebled health, might take a winter's trip to the Riviera, or to the recuperative sands of the Sahara?

The article was indeed a scathing arraignment, a masterpiece of ridicule, but as it went on it became even worse, for it now got down to the making of serious charges against my son's integrity.

"Such are the alleged purposes of this project," said *The Gad.* "Let us now consider its real purpose, far more insidious than anyone has hitherto suspected, but which is now seen to be that of *separating the widows and orphans of this land from their accumulated savings,* and diverting them into the *pockets of Noah and his family!*"

I thought I should sink through the floor when this met my eyes, and I was appalled when I read on and realized how many thousands of people would believe the plausible tale of villainy *The Gad* had managed to construct out of a few innocent facts. Noah's plan was in brief stated to be a scheme for the impoverishment of innocent investors, by selling them shares of stock, both common and preferred, in his International Marine and Zoo Flotation Company. According to the writer of this infamous libel, immediately the vessel was finished at a cost of about $79.50, it was Noah's intention to incorporate his enterprise with himself as President and Treasurer, and Shem, Ham and Japhet as his Board of Directors, the capital being placed at the enormous sum of $100,000,000.

"This capitalization," said the exposure, "will be divided into fifty millions of preferred stock, and fifty millions of common, all of which will be sold to the public at par; subject to a first mortgage already existing, and held by Noah and his sons, which it is intended to foreclose, and the company reorganized, the minute the $100,000,000 of the public's money has passed into the treasurer's hands.

"Talk about your *deluge!*" continued the article. "This is indeed the biggest thing in *deluges* this little old world has ever known. The Preadamite Steel Trust is a dewdrop alongside of it. Noah gets the *salvage,* but the *people* get the *water!*"

Such was the attitude of the public toward my son's great project, and all I could ever get him to say in reply to these and other equally nefarious charges was, while he had intended to have quarters for every kind of beast on board his boat, he had now definitely decided to leave out Mastodons, Muck-Rakers and Yellow Journalists!

Verily there seems to be some foundation to the belief that devotion to the life of a seaman makes a man callous to assaults on his personal reputation!

Chapter VIII

ON THE EXTINCTION OF THE MASTODON

The recent visit of King Ptush to our wild districts in search of a fresh hunting-ground for himself and his son, Prince Ptutt, brought about a very serious condition of affairs in respect to the mastodon, or what some persons refer to as the Antediluvians. This most distinguished personage, wearying of the affairs of state in his own land, gave over the reins of government for a while to his Grand Vizier, and on behalf of the Nimrodian Institution, a Museum of Natural and Unnatural History in his own capital city, came hither to study the fauna and flora of our district, and incidentally to take back with him a variety of stuffed specimens of our more conspicuous wild beasts for exhibition purposes. Entirely unaware of His Majesty's unerring aim in hitting large surfaces at short range, we welcomed him cordially to our midst, and rather unwisely presented him with the freedom of the jungle, a ceremony which carried with it the privilege of bagging anything he could hit with his slungshot, in season or out of it. The results of His Majesty's visit were appalling, for he had not been with us more than six weeks before his enthusiasm getting the better of his sportsmanship he turned the jungle into a zoological shambles, from which it is never likely to recover. On his first day's outing, to our dismay he brought down thirty-seven ring-tailed ornithorhyncusses, eighteen pterodactyls, three brace of dodo, and a domesticated diplodocus, and then assured us that he didn't know what could be the matter with his aim that he had missed so many. The next day he rose early, and while the rest of his suite were sleeping went out unattended, returning before breakfast was over with a tally-card showing a killing of thirteen dinosaurs, twenty-seven megatheriums, and about six tons of chlamy-dophori, not to mention a mammoth jack-rabbit that some idiot had told him was the only specimen in the world of the monodelphian mollycoddle. The situation became very embarrassing to us because we were on excellent terms with King Ptush and his subjects, and we did not wish to do anything to offend either of them, but here was a case where in the interests of our own fauna something had to be done. Going on at the rate in which he had begun it was easy to see that unless somebody got out an injunction restraining him from shooting between meals it would not be many days before there wasn't a prehistoric beast left in the whole country. It was a mighty ticklish position for all of us. If we withdrew the freedom of the jungle His Majesty might go home in a huff and declare war against us, and with Noah's Ark as the sum total of our navy, and that built in a ten-acre lot thirty miles from the coast, and no army of any sort standing or sitting, we could hardly afford a complication of that kind. Our wisest counselors were called together to consider the situation, but they were all men given to many words and lovers of disputation, so that what with the framing of the original resolution, and the time consumed in debating the amendments offered thereto, it was quite three months before any definite conclusion was reached, and it was then found when the resolution came up to its final vote that it had nothing whatever to do with the subject the conference was called to discuss, but had been transformed into an Act providing for an increased duty on guinea-pigs imported from Sumatra. From that day to this I have had little belief in that kind of popular government which provides for the election of public servants whose chief end and aim seems to be to thwart the public will.

It was then that my fellow-citizens, availing themselves of a certain diplomacy of method which I was said to possess, called upon me to undertake a personal interview with King Ptush, and to see what could be done to stay his voracious appetite for the slaying of our mammalia. Always ready to serve my fellows in their hour of need, I undertook the mission, and appeared bright and early one morning at his encampment, unannounced, thinking it better to seem to happen in upon him in a neighborly fashion than to make a national affair of my mission by coming formally and with official pomp into his presence. At the hour of my arrival the great king was standing on the stump of a red cedar, delivering a lecture to his entourage upon "The Whole Duty of Man, With a Few Remarks About Everything Else." But even then he was not neglectful of his opportunities as a Nimrod, for every now and then he would punctuate his sentences with a shot at a casual bit of fauna passing by, either on the earth or flying, never pausing in his lecture, but nevertheless bringing to an untimely end thirty-eight griffins, seven paralellopipedon, a gumshurhynicus, forty google-eyed plutocratidæ, and a herd of June-bugs grazing in a neighboring pasture – the latter wholly domesticated, by the way, and used by their owner as spile-drivers for a dike he was building in apprehension of Noah's predicted flood. It was then that I began to get some insight into the character of this wonderful person, for as I sat there listening to his discourse, delivered at the rate of five hundred words a minute, and apparently covering seven or eight subjects not necessarily corollary or collateral to each other, at once, and watched him simultaneously bringing down with unerring aim this tremendous bag of game, something of the man's intrinsic nature was revealed to me. His strength, of which we had heard much from travelers in his own land, lay in an almost scientific lack of concentration, backed up by a vocabulary of tremendous scope, and a condition of optical near-sightedness that enabled him to see but obscurely further than the end of his nose. These attributes gave him the power to discuss innumerable subjects coeternally, if not coherently, using his vocabulary with such skill that his meaning depended entirely upon the interpretation of his remarks by individual hearers, while the limitations of vision caused him, on the sudden appearance of masses of any sort, to shoot at them impulsively, regardless of such minor details as consequences. As a result of these gifts he was ever hitting something with either the arrows of speech or the slungshot, which produced a public impression of ceaseless activity and of material accomplishment. In addition to this it was his wont to do all things smiling with an almost boyish manifestation of pleasure, so that he endeared himself to the people and was pronounced in some respects likeable even by his enemies.

When his lecture was over he descended from his improvised platform and greeted me most cordially.

"Deeee-lighted!" was the exact word he used as he took my hand and shook it until my arm worked indifferently well in its socket.

I was not aware that His Highness had ever heard of me before, but it was not long before I was more than glad that I had come, for it transpired that I was the one person in all creation that he had most wished to meet, though for what particular purpose he did not make clear. In any event, so cordial was his reception of me that for three or four weeks I had not the heart to mention the particular object of my mission, and even then I was not permitted to do so because at any time when I felt that the psychological moment had been reached he would talk of other things, his scientific lack of concentration of which I have already spoken enabling him with much grace to be reminded of an experience in the Transvaal by a chance allusion of my own to the peculiar habits of the Antillean Sardine. In the meanwhile the work of slaughter was going on apace, and whole species were gradually becoming extinct. Exactly five weeks after my arrival the last Diplodocus in the world breathed its last. Two days later the world's visible supply of Pterodactyls passed into the realms of the annihilated. The Dodo, the largest and sweetest song-bird I have ever known, the only bird in all the primeval forests possessed of a diaphragm capable of expressing harmonies of what for want of a better term I may call a Wagnerian range, quickly followed suit, and in its train, alas! went the others, Creosauri, Dicosauri, Thracheotomi, Megacheropodæ, Manicuridæ, and the Willumjay, the latter a gigantic parrot with a voice like silver that rang continuously through the forests like a huge fire bell. At the end of the tenth week of my mission a message was received from Noah.

"Dear Grandpa," he wrote:

"Can't you do something to stave off King Ptush? In making up my passenger-list I can't get hold of enough mammals to fill an inside room. I have been through the country with a fine-tooth comb, and as far as I can find out there isn't a prehistoric beast left in creation. If this thing goes on much longer I shall be compelled to load up with a cargo of coon-cats, armadillos, hippopotami and Plymouth rocks. Get a move on!

"NOAH"

My first impulse was to hand this letter without a word to His Majesty, but on second thoughts I decided not to do this, since it might involve me in a humiliating explanation of my grandson's foolish obsession about the impending flood. I had too much pride to wish King Ptush to know that I had a human brainstorm on the list of my posterity, so I threw the brick upon which the letter was engraved into a neighboring fishpond, and resolved to get rid of His Majesty by strategy. For three nights I pondered over my plan of operations, and then the great method came to me like the dawning of the sun after a night of abysmal darkness. I went to the royal tent and discovered His Majesty hard at work chiseling out an article on "How I Brought Down My First Proterosaurus" on a slab of granite he had brought with him. As I approached he smiled broadly, and with a wave of his hand called my attention to the previous day's bag. It covered a ten-acre lot.

"There isn't sawdust enough in creation to stuff half of these beasts," he remarked proudly. "I hardly know what I shall do about that."

"Better bury them in the mud," I suggested, "and let them petrify."

He seemed pleased with the idea, and later put it into operation.

"Fossils are not so susceptible to moths," he observed as he gave orders for their immersion in a Triassic mud-puddle of huge proportions. "That was a good idea of yours, Methuselah."

"I have a better one than that," I returned, seeing at last an opening for my strategic movement. "Why should a man of Your Majesty's prowess waste his time on such insignificant creatures as these, when the whole country is ringing with complaints of an animal a thousand times as large, and that no one hereabouts has ever dared attempt to pursue?"

He was on the alert instantly.

"What animal do you refer to?" he demanded, his interest becoming so deep that he put four pairs of eyeglasses upon his royal nose, so that he could see me better.

"It belongs to the family of Rodents," I replied. "It is without any exception the biggest rat in the history of our mammals. It is a combination of the Castoridæ, the Chinchillidæ, the Dodgastidæ, and the Lagomydian Leporidæ, with just a dash of the Dippydoodle on the maternal side."

His Majesty gave a sigh of disappointment, and resumed his writing.

"I haven't come here to shoot rats," he observed coldly, removing the three extra pairs of spectacles from his nose. "I am a huntsman, not a trapper."

"Your Majesty does not understand that this is no ordinary rat," I returned calmly. "If I may be permitted to continue, what would Your Highness think of a rat that was several thousand feet higher than the pyramids, that has lived continuously for thousands of years, and is as fresh and green in spirit as on the day it was born? Suppose I were to tell you that so great is its strength that I have myself seen a whole herd of aboriginal elephants lying asleep upon its broad back? What would you say if I told you that its epidermis is so thick that if there were such a thing as a steam-drill in creation six hundred of them could bore away at it night and day for as many years without making any visible impression thereon?"

He again put down his chisel, and laid the hammer aside, as he ranged the extra eyeglasses along the bridge of his nose.

"Colonel Methuselah," he said, incisively biting off his words, "if you told me anything of the kind I should say that you are what posterity will probably call a nature faker, and one of a perniciously invidious sort."

"I can bring affidavits to prove it, Your Majesty," said I.

"It is strange that I have never heard of it before," he mused.

"We are not particularly proud of it," I explained. "One may boast of the number of Discosauri one finds in one's hunting preserves, or the marvelous fish in one's lakes, or the birds of wondrous plumage that dwell in one's forests, but none ever ventures to speak of the number or quality of rats that infest the locality."

"You say it overtops a pyramid?" he demanded.

"I do," I replied. "The exact estimate of its height is sixteen thousand nine hundred and sixty-four feet!"

"Great Snakes!" he cried. "Why, he must be a perfect mountain!"

"He is," I replied. "He is so tall that summer and winter the top of his head is covered with snow."

This was too much for King Ptush. He rose up immediately from his seat and summoned his entourage.

"You will make ready for a strenuous afternoon," he said to them sharply. "I am going after the biggest game that history records. Colonel Methuselah has just told me of a quarry alongside of which all that we have landed in the past months sinks into insignificance."

"You do well to call it a quarry," I cried. "There never was a better – and it is only ten miles from here as the griffin flies."

The king's face flushed with joy at the prospect, but suddenly a look of perplexity came into his eyes.

"By the way," he said, "how shall we bring him down – with a slungshot or a catapult?"

I laughed.

"No ordinary ammunition will serve Your Majesty's purpose here," I said. "The only thing for you to do is to steal quietly up to him while he sleeps. Surround him in the silence of some black night, and build a barbed-wire fence around him. Once you succeed in doing this he will not try to get away, and you can have him removed at Your Majesty's pleasure."

"We go at once," cried the king, his enthusiasm aroused to the highest pitch. "My friends," he added, drawing himself up to the full of his soldierly height, "we go to capture the – the – the er – by the way, Colonel, what do you call this creature?"

"The Ararat," I replied.

He repeated the word after me, sprang lightly into the saddle of Griffin we had presented to him upon his arrival, and, followed by his entourage, was off on the greatest hunt of his life. What happened subsequently we never knew, for none of the party ever returned; but what I do know is that my stratagem came too late.

A subsequent investigation of our preserves showed that all our treasured mastodons from the Jurassic, Triassic, and other periods of history, had been killed off, root, stock and branch, by our honored guest, and poor Noah was reduced to the necessity of drumming up trade among such commonplace creatures as the Rhinoceri, the Yak, the Dromedary, and that vain but ornamental combination of fuss and feathers known as the Hen.

The Ararat we still have with us, and as for me, I am inclined to think that it will remain, flood or no flood, for any creature that has successfully withstood a campaign against it by King Ptush cannot be removed from the scene by anything short of a convulsion of Nature.

Chapter IX

(This Chapter of the Autobiography of Methuselah is made up entirely of fragments. The manuscript of the preceding chapters was found in fine condition, and entirely unobliterated by the passage of the centuries since it was written, but beginning at this point cracks appear, and in some places such complete fractures as make the continuity of the narrative impossible. The fragments have been as carefully deciphered as the complete chapters, however, and are here presented for what they are worth.)

AS TO WOMEN

The position of woman among us will doubtless prove of interest to posterity. Our matrimonial laws are not all that they should be, in my judgment, though there are men who consider them as nearly perfect as they can be made. The idea that the best way for a young man to declare his love for a young girl is to hit her on the head with a wooden club and then run off with her before she regains consciousness has never received my approval, and never will. Something should be left for the post-nuptial life, and I cannot see how after it has been used as an instrument of courtship a club can take its place as it ought to as an instrument of discipline in the household. My own wives I have invariably caught in a trap, so that later on in life, when I have found it desirable to emphasize my authority in my home by means of a stout stick, that emblem of power has had no glamour about it to weaken its force as an argument. . . . Then as to the number of wives that a man should be permitted to have, I am in distinct disagreement with the majority of my neighbors, who maintain that it is entirely a matter of individual choice as to whether a man should have five, ten or a thousand. I should not advocate the limitation to an arbitrary number, but I believe that the question of one's actual needs should rule. If a man's possessions enable him to maintain a large establishment requiring the services of a cook, a laundress, two waitresses and four upstairs girls, eight wives would be sufficient; but on the other hand, for a young man beginning his career who needs only a general house-worker, one is enough. Individual cases should regulate the law as applied to the individual, and those who claim that they may marry any number of women, whether they need them or not, entirely regardless of whether or not they can keep them occupied, should be told that no man is entitled to more of the good things of this life than he can avail himself of in his daily procedure. Any other course than this will sooner or later result in a great scarcity of nuptial raw material, and it is not impossible to conceive of a day when all the women in the land will become the property of a select, privileged few. A monopoly of this sort would enable a few men to control posterity and build up a Trust in the Matrimonial Industry that would engender not only a great deal of bitter feeling between the masses and the classes, but enforce a system of compulsory bachelorhood which . . . Nevertheless, if woman wants to vote let her do so. In spite of all that I have just said about the subtle quality of her intellect, I still say let her vote. What harm can come from permitting her to go to the polls and drop a ballot in the box for this or that man, or for this or that measure? It will please her to be allowed to do this, and by granting her petition for the suffrage we shall put an end to an otherwise endless disputation. I am quite sure that as long as her votes are kept separate from the men's votes, and are *not* counted, no possible harm can come from a little complacency in the face of . . . Personally I have no objection to divorce. If a man marries a woman under the impression that she is a good cook, and after the waning of the honeymoon finds that she does not know the difference between sponge-cake and a plain common garden sponge, why should he be forced forevermore to court dyspepsia on her account? I fail to see either justice or reason in this, though as to the method of divorce I cannot agree with those who claim that as the man has married the woman by hitting her with a club, as I have already shown, the proper method of divorce is for the woman to return the blow with a rolling-pin. The proper way to do is for the husband to be permitted to return the girl to her parents as not up to the specifications, or if she have no parents to dispose of her at the best bargain possible to one of his neighbors who may happen to be in need of a girl of that sort at that particular time. . . . But these Newport separations, as I believe they are called, are apt to prove embarrassing, particularly when the divorcées all happen to be present at the same dinner-table. A lady whose hostess is the wife of her former husband, finding herself sitting opposite the divorced wife of her present husband, who has at one time or another been married to two or three other ladies at the board, is not likely to be able to comport herself with that degree of *savoir faire* that is the earmark of the refined. . . .

As for the mother-in-law, for certain reasons of a private nature I was not going to speak of her in these memoirs, but after mature reflection upon the subject I deem it my duty to posterity to say that. . . .

SOME LONG-FELT WANTS

I have often wished that in my youth I had studied science a little more carefully. It is growing very obvious to me the longer I live that there are a number of little things that we need in this world to make life more comfortable. It does not seem to me beyond reason to think that by the use of a proper mechanism these thunderbolts that play about the heavens can be made to do errands for us. It angers me to see so much light going to waste in the heavens from the flash of the lightning, when it might be stored up for use instead of these intolerable axle-grease dips that we are forced to use to light us on our way to bed. I don't see why someone cannot entrap one of these bolts on a wire, just as we catch a rat in a trap, and keep it running round and round a loop, giving out its light until it is exhausted. . . . It would be pleasant, too, to have a kind of carriage that would go of its own power. I cannot quite reason the thing out, but I believe that the time will come when there will be something of the sort. I remember back in my four-hundred-and-fifty-second year finding one of my father's farm wagons on the top of the hill back of the cow pasture. I wheeled it to the edge of the descent, and was much delighted to see it go speeding down to the base of the hill, gathering momentum at every turn of the wheels, and ending up by hitting the back door of Uncle Zibb's cottage with such force that it came out of the front parlor window before stopping. This seemed to indicate that under certain circumstances a wheeled vehicle could be made to go without a horse, but in what precise way it can be brought about the limitations of my mechanical training prevent me from determi . . . I was watching the heated vapor rising from our tea-kettle the other night, and was much diverted to notice that it made a whistling sort of sound as it emerged from the nozzle of the pot. It ran from B sharp to high C, and was loud enough to be heard on the other side of the room. It has occurred to me that there may be in this some hidden principle that will some day enable man to make this vapor do his work for him, especially along musical lines. Surely if this misty substance can make a tea-kettle squeak, why should it not, if multiplied in volume and run through a trombone, afford us a capable substitute for Bill Watkins, who plays second base on our Village Band?

AS TO PROPHECIES

If our Prophets would only confine themselves to probabilities I am inclined to think we should take more stock in the things they foretell. I am impelled to the making of this reflection by the presence in our town of an Astrologer who is setting all the women by the ears by prophesying a day when they will not have to do their own housework, and will thrive in many lines of endeavor now open solely to men. He is an interesting old fellow, in spite of the foolishness of his predictions; but when he tells the women's clubs that in some far off century women will be found writing novels, and adorning themselves with rich fabrics, and surrounded by a class of paid toilers who will do nothing but minister to their ease and comfort, I lose all patience with him. It is filling their minds with socialistic notions that are impairing their usefulness, and I have had to chastise seven of my own fair helpmeets this past week for neglecting their duties and treating my instructions with contempt. A curious thing about his prophecies is their confirmation of Adam's fears as to the ultimate result of these new-fangled ideas as to dress, and, what interested me more than anything else, he predicted a machine called a Moh-Thor-Cah, that not only runs along without outside assistance, but is propelled entirely by the same vapor that I have spoken of before as striking the high C in the nozzle of my tea-kettle. He goes too far with this, as well as with his other prophecies, for he says that there will be a time when ships larger than Noah's Ark will be forced across great bodies of water by this same power. The idea of anybody, after Noah's experience, being foolish enough to build a craft of that kind, to say nothing of working it with a tea-kettle, is preposterously abs . . . In one of his visions he claims to have seen a gathering of people, called a city, in which there are to be more than four million souls, and governed not by the virtuous, as in our own day, but by the most desperate political malefactors that ever banded together for plunder, and this at the direct request of the people themselves! I am perfectly aware that human nature is weak, and given over at times to strange delusions, but that any body of self-respecting persons should deliberately and of their own free will turn the management of their affairs over to those who would more properly grace a jail than a City Hall, surpasses belie . . .

MISCELLANEOUS FRAGMENTS

. . . cannot be denied that a daily newspaper would be an interesting thing, if it were possible to print it, but I doubt its real value. I dislike gossip, and I do not see how the newspaper could fill up without it. What advantage is it to me to know that Hiram Wigglesworth, of Ararat Corners, who is unknown to me, was arrested on Thursday evening for beating his wife? Why should I be called upon to impair the value of my eyes by reading in small type all the scandalous details of the separation proceedings between two people I never saw and would not permit to enter my front door if they came to call? It is nothing to me that Mrs. Zebulon Zebedee, of Enochsville, has spent thirty thousand clam-shells a year on bottled grape-juice, and run up bills against her husband's account at the diamond-quarries for two or three hundred thousand tons of wampum, and if she chooses to go joy-riding on a Diplodocus with a gentleman from the Circus, it is Zebulon Zebedee's business, not mine, and a newspaper that insisted upon dumping this unsavory mess on my breakfast-table every morning would sooner or later become an unmitigated nuis . . .

*

. . .But he pays no attention to my protestations. I think the old-time method of walloping them every Sunday morning, on the principle that they deserved it for something they had done during the past week, was a good one. Shem and Japhet are not so bad, but since Ham came back from the Ararat Academy of Higher Learning he has been about as useless a member of the community as we have ever had. What he doesn't know would fill six hundred volumes of the Triassic Cyclopædia. I caught him only the other night trying to teach his grandmother to suck eggs, although my estimable wife was a past-mistress of that art four hundred years before he was born. He has absolutely no respect for age, and frequently refers to me as "the old boy," criticizes my clothes, and remarks apropos of my patriarchal garments that night-shirts as an article of dress for a five o'clock tea went out a thousand years ago. Indeed, so disrespectful is he that I sometimes wonder if he is not a foundling. I note two suspicious things in respect to him. The first is that he is getting blacker in the face every day, which suggests that there is in him somewhere a strain of the

Æthiopian, none of which he gets from me or his grandmother, who was an Albino. And the second is that his father will not allow him to be spanked, a very strange inhibition, I think, unless that operation would disclose the boy's possession of the Missing Link. Indeed, I should not be at all surprised to discover that the lad is either an Æthiopian, or a direct descendant of Adam's old friend and neighbor, Col. Darwin J. Simian, of Coacoa-on-Nut. In all of my reflections on the subject of the training of the young, manual training has always seemed to me the most efficacious, especially if in applying the hand you do not restrain its force, and are not loath to use the hair-brush or a good leathern trunk-strap as an auxiliary. And in order to ensure their freedom from evil associations, and to keep them from making the night hideous by their raucous yells, I have never heard of anything better than the method of Doctor Magog Rodd, of the Enochsville Military Academy, who kept his students in cages and corked them up every night before they retir . . .

*

. . . So no more at present. My manuscript already weighs three hundred and forty tons, and every word of it has been gouged out with my own hands – a difficult operation for a man of my years. I am painfully aware of its shortcomings, but such as it is it is, and so it must remain. There is no time left for its revision, and, indeed, a man who has just celebrated his nine hundred and sixty-ninth birthday can hardly be expected . . .

www.ingramcontent.com/pod-product-compliance
Lightning Source LLC
LaVergne TN
LVHW101322110826
845152LV00011B/31
* 9 7 8 1 6 0 6 6 4 5 9 6 3 *